THE TRUTH ABOUT FAME

Faith & Fortune 2

TONI SHILOH

Praise for *The Trouble With Love*

"In her iconic soulful fashion, Toni Shiloh has penned another heartfelt page-turner…this time with a dash of suspense thrown in!"

- Sarah Monzon, award-winning author of *Finders Keepers*

"Swoony, sweet and a little sassy, *The Trouble With Love* is Toni Shiloh's best novel yet! A beautiful story of friendship, romance, and brokenness meeting grace."

- Carrie Schmidt, Reading is My SuperPower

"In *The Trouble With Love*, Toni Shiloh offers a fresh take on modern romance that will twirl you about the New York City high life, yet still manages to keep the characters completely relatable with their fears, longings, and faith struggles. The romance between Holiday and Emmett is flirty, fun, and completely squeal-inducing. Enjoy this escape from everyday life and dive into Shiloh's world of faith and fortune!"

– Janine Rosche, author of This Wandering Heart

THE TRUTH ABOUT FAME

By
Toni Shiloh

Scripture taken from the New King James Version®. Copyright © 1982 by Thomas Nelson. Used by permission. All rights reserved.

Exodus 14:14 taken from the Holy Bible, New International Version®, NIV®, Copyright © 1973, 1978, 1984, 2011 by Biblical, Inc.® Used by permission. All rights reserved worldwide.

Edited by Katie Donovan.

Cover design by Toni Shiloh.

Cover art photos © Shutterstock.com/Gorbash Varvara used by permission.

Published in the United States of America by Toni Shiloh.

www.ToniShiloh.com

The Truth About Fame is a work of fiction. Names, characters, places, and incidents are either products of the author's imagination or used fictitiously. All characters are fictional, and any similarity to people living or dead is purely coincidental.

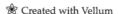 Created with Vellum

DEDICATION

To the Author and Finisher of my faith.

LIFE—A NIGHTMARE I COULDN'T WAKE FROM.

Shooting up to the highest echelons of fame had ensured I'd gained a wide following, which no doubt included a few individuals appearing on the FBI's Most Wanted list or some government's watch list. But honestly, I never thought a stalker would wreck my world and earn me constant protection.

Of course, earning the title of *supermodel* added a special kind of twist, because men who saw me in magazines assumed that look in my eyes was meant for them. Never mind that the photographer had been shouting commands nonstop, seeking the best photo. The one that would continue their success—and mine—in the fashion industry. Still, men wanted the illusions my look brought and more.

Despite what most people thought, fame wasn't all it was cracked up to be.

For the past few months, my life had been like a night terror that left me silently screaming. My reaction had to be silent, because if my friends knew just how close I was to falling apart, they'd put their lives on hold until mine was better. I couldn't let them do that, especially considering Holiday was now engaged to my brother, Emmett.

The happy occasion should have left me ecstatic instead of plotting my escape. What choice did I have? I needed to leave. To get far away. If I wasn't here in my Manhattan townhouse, then my roomies (aka best friends) would be safe.

I looked around my fourth-floor bedroom for any items I wanted to take with me. My gaze paused on the gold-colored curtains that lent a richness to the room that had been my sanctuary. They went perfectly with the cream-colored Egyptian sheets and duvet that welcomed and lulled me to sleep on a nightly basis. Wherever I ended up probably wouldn't have such a great thread count, nor the gold twinkling chandelier that hung from the center of the ceiling. But I'd readily leave the glamour behind if it meant safety for the people I cared about.

If I wanted to hide and keep others safe, then I had to go someplace no one would expect. Someplace contrary to the opulence of my everyday life. A place where I could blend in with the masses.

I pulled the black duffel bag from beneath my king-sized bed. A few days ago, when the idea first sprouted, I'd gone and purchased items that would help me sneak away. And although I couldn't truly escape life, I needed an opportunity to focus and regroup in a relatively safe location. A lot of people would lose their minds once I revealed my desire to step back from modeling and social obligations, but I didn't plan on spilling the beans until I was far, *far* away.

The bottom of the duffel had already been lined with the new sneakers, jeans, and T-shirts I'd bought. I threw in my Yankees cap and a few wigs. Yesterday, I'd dyed my blonde pixie to a more natural mahogany color. The brown shade was more in keeping with my African American heritage. Some people thought it was ridiculous for a Black woman to dye her hair blonde, but I rocked the look. My hair stylist had first recommended it when I'd done a shoot to create my modeling portfolio. The hair coupled with my blue-green eyes probably earned me more jobs than I could count.

Right now, I needed the darker shade to keep people from giving me a second look and guessing where they'd seen me before. And if that didn't work, the black and other colored wigs in my bag would surely help. No one could know I was Tori Bell, supermodel and daughter to famed actors Theo and Jackie Bell.

A rap of knuckles at my bedroom door startled me. I swallowed, pulling for a confident voice. "Yes?"

"I need to talk to you."

I bristled at the sound of Fox's—the thorn-in-my-side security guard's—voice. Granted, he'd kept me safe in a car accident last month. He'd broken his wrist, while I'd merely walked away with a few cuts and bruises. I felt my face contort in a wince.

Okay, so Fox wasn't all *that* bad. Still, his insistence that the accident had been purely coincidental grated on my nerves. What were the odds that a woman with a stalker would just happen to get hit by someone else?

I pulled on the blonde wig that went to my shoulders and then opened the door. "What?"

He rolled his eyes. "Nice to see you too."

Some days I would very much agree that it was nice to see him. After all, he had rugged good looks, courtesy of a bald head—whether because he was actually balding or because he knew it made him look fierce, I hadn't figured out yet—and dark-chocolate skin that made me think of my favorite Amedi chocolate bar. Then he'd go and open his mouth, ruining the illusion.

"I'm busy, so make it fast." I popped a hand on my hip, staring him down.

"May I come in, or would you rather your roommates hear us?"

Curiosity pecked at me. What could he possibly have to say that I wouldn't want Holiday and Octavia to hear? I stepped back and motioned him in toward the sitting area.

He raised an eyebrow and curled a lip at the pair of shell-back French chairs. "I'll just stand."

"Fine." I folded my arms. "What do you have to say?"

"I can offer you a place of refuge."

"Say what now?" The irritation that chafed me every time he was around gave way to surprise.

"You've got *flight* written all over your face, Princess. Don't act like you're not planning to run away."

Okay, maybe I was too quick to let go of my annoyance. Fox had a way of getting to me, making me feel like a porcupine poised for a fight. I tried to hold my face expressionless as I responded. "You do *not* know me."

"Whatever, Princess." He matched my stance. "Do you want a place to stay or not?"

Just because he was behaving like a Neanderthal, didn't mean I had to respond in kind.

I took a breath. "Depends," I said cautiously. "How far away is this place?" Like, did I need to grab my passport?

"Queens."

My eyes started an arc, and I had to freeze them to keep them from rolling all the way. "That's too close. I thought you were going to suggest the other side of the country or even *out* of the country."

"I'm not a millionaire like some people I know." He gave me a pointed look.

Fair enough. "What makes you think I'd be safe?"

"Do you really think someone would go looking for you in Queens?"

Okay, he had a point. "Is it a safe house?"

"In a sense."

"Fox, you're killing me with the cryptic talk." I rolled my

4

hand in a continue motion. "Break it down and just spit it out."

"My grandmother lives in a two-bedroom apartment."

I blanched. "You'd put your grandma in danger? You can stay with her."

His jaw pulsed. "Do you seriously think she doesn't already have a top-notch security system? I own a security company, for goodness' sake."

I sighed and flopped into a chair, rubbing the tension pounding the middle of my forehead. "I don't think that's a good idea."

A rustle of movement caught my attention, and I watched as Fox grimaced, lowering himself into the chair opposite from me. He looked really uncomfortable, as if he were afraid he'd break the antique. If my head weren't hurting so much, I'd find the situation amusing.

"Look, Princess. I can take better care of you at my grandmother's. No one will think to look for you there. And I have a feeling you won't be telling Ms. Brown or Ms. Ricci. It'll help us know if the incident involving Ms. Brown and your brother was a fluke or…"

"Or all my fault." I gulped, remembering how horrified I'd been to find out Emmett had been shot. He'd been at the concert to watch Holiday sing with her father at Madison Square Garden. Law enforcement thought Holiday was the intended target, but still I wondered, especially when Emmett —being Emmett—took a bullet for her.

Did he get hurt because of me?

"Are you sure your grandmother won't mind?"

"She loves company. She'll be delighted."

I stared into his inky black eyes. "And you? You'll continue to guard me?" Which hadn't been my original idea, but I couldn't help admitting the thought made me breathe a little easier.

"That's what I agreed to do and what your father's paying me for. This'll make my job a lot easier." He held up a hand. "But don't let that make you stay here. No need to be difficult."

I almost cracked a smile. Instead, I pursed my lips so I wouldn't give in to his humor. "Fine. I'll go."

"Good. I'll let her know you're coming. Your roommates are going out soon. We can leave shortly after they do, so they won't know."

"Right." I stood. "I'm almost done packing, then I'll be ready."

"I'll wait for you downstairs." He gave a satisfied smirk before closing the door quietly behind him.

What had I just agreed to?

❧ 2 ❧

FOX DECIDED TO DRIVE ME TO HIS GRANDMOTHER'S APARTMENT instead of using one of our chauffeurs. Logically, it made sense, but still. I couldn't remember the last time I'd sat up front in a vehicle. Having a clear view of the scenery before me was almost as exciting as all the buttons on the dashboard. The desire to reach out and touch them, to regulate the temperature—out of nerves, not necessity—had me sitting on my hands instead. I felt a little bit like a child.

If that wasn't enough to bombard my senses, the quietness in the interior was too...too loud. Fox hadn't said a peep since he'd started driving. Sometimes I wondered if he clammed up just to annoy me. He had an uncanny way of reading me and acting in a way that got *right* on my nerves.

"Say something," I blurted as he took the exit toward Queens.

"What exactly do you want me to say?"

I could practically hear the smirk in his voice, but I refused to look at his face for confirmation. That and I didn't want him to think I cared if I amused him.

"Anything. I can't take the quiet."

Inwardly, I shook my head. Why did I have to tell the truth? *Don't lower your guard, Tori.*

"How long have you known Ms. Brown and Ms. Ricci?"

My head jerked backward. Of all the things he could have asked, that certainly hadn't been on my playlist of possibilities.

"What? You told me to talk, so I'm talking." His voice was as masculine as his muscles. It was a little annoying, his physical perfection. Surely he had a flaw somewhere.

Oh, wait. He had plenty. I sighed and refocused. "Since we were thirteen. We went to the same boarding school."

"People really send their kids away for school?"

I chuckled. "Yes, and they were the only two girls I really liked."

"Why's that?"

"We had the richest parents, so we knew none of us were being overly friendly just to suck up to one another." And what a relief it had been to be able to relax in front of someone for a change and not wonder whether my opinions would end up on the tabloids or the school's social gossip mill. "Even when people have money, they still try and brownnose." Not the word I wanted to use, but I was working on my language.

"I can only imagine."

"Oh, the tales I could tell." I threw him a sardonic gaze, quickly shifting my eyes forward again when he studied me a little *too* closely.

Fox had an awfully bad habit of watching me. I couldn't decide if it was because I was a model, rich, or something else entirely too terrifying to mull over. He observed me as if I were some specimen under a microscope, and by examining me, he'd have me all figured out.

"All right, I'm game." His voice broke the silence once more. "Tell me the funniest tale from school."

Hmm. I searched through my memories for a whopper. "Oh! I've got one." I shifted, angling myself toward the driver's seat. "Every homecoming, the school would pick a board member to honor. They'd show up, say a few words, and everyone would try to rub elbows with that person."

He nodded. "I'm tracking so far."

"So, one year my mom was picked."

"She's on that soap opera, right?"

I snorted. "That soap opera?" *Really*? Jacqueline Bell was a soap opera legend, having won Emmy after Emmy after Emmy. Not to mention the Tony Awards she racked up every time she stepped foot on Broadway. She was in the midst of rehearsals right now, hoping for the next Broadway hit. I was honestly surprised *she* wasn't the one with a stalker.

Fox shrugged. "I don't have time to watch a lot of TV. I just recognized her because my grandmother loves her show."

"Well, yeah. She's won awards and such." And promptly wrapped them and placed them in a box. I hadn't yet asked what she intended to do with them. Hock them on eBay? Not that she needed the money.

"So, what happened when they announced her as the honoree?"

"I had classmates knocking on my door every few minutes. Octavia ended up leaving to go practice at the campus ballet studio because the constant knocking was ruining her concentration."

"And Ms. Brown?"

I shook my head. "She just sat on her bed holding in the laughter with each knock. Well, someone knocked *again,* and I answered to see last year's homecoming queen dressed up in an outfit that tugged at the corner of a memory."

"Go on."

"She was wearing a red dress and had dyed her hair

brown—she was actually a blonde white girl—and then it dawned on me. She had dressed up as my mom in a famous scene of hers from *Days Gone By*. Thank goodness she'd enough sense not to bronze her skin."

"What did you do?"

The hint of amusement in Fox's voice made the memory all the fresher. "The only thing I could do." I shrugged, a mischievous smile tugging at the corners of my lips. "Took a selfie with her and posted it online as a 'who wore it better?'"

Fox's rich laughter filled the interior, and I wanted to pat myself on the back. This was probably the most cordial conversation we'd ever had. It wasn't that I didn't want to be cordial; I just hated that I needed a bodyguard. It was so 1990s and cliché. I mean, yes, celebrities had to use security at times, but I wasn't a member of Congress. I wasn't the president of the United States. Having 24/7 security rankled and made me want to strike out in rebellion. Thus, the reason my snarky side came out with Fox often the target.

Add the fact he was a man and called me *Princess*, and my snark was practically justified.

"Did you like going to boarding school?"

His question broke through my inner diatribe. How honest did I want to be? I didn't want to give Fox any ammunition to use against me later.

"You don't have to answer. I was just doing as you asked and talking."

I peeked at him, studying his profile. The strength in his jaw. In his muscles. In *him*. As much as I didn't want him around, he'd protected me. Kept me safe. I owed him now.

"Not really." There. To the point and not incriminating. "What about you? What was growing up like for you?"

He glanced at me as if assessing my motives. "I grew up in Queens and was raised by my grandmother. She took my sister and me in. Made sure we were loved, and wanted for nothing. She gave us a good life."

Yet so much was missing from his story. Like, where were his parents? How old was he when he first moved in with his grandmother? I wanted to ask but didn't want the give and take that would be required of me in that type of conversation.

So, I settled for the simple route. "Are we going to the home you grew up in? Or did your grandmother move once you guys moved out?"

"Same home. She says the only way she'll leave is in a casket."

I laughed. "Morbid, but I like her sass."

"Oh, she has that in spades."

I studied him. Not a hint of gray in his lined and trimmed beard, but there was a maturity about him that said he was older than my twenty-seven years. "How old are you, Fox?"

"Thirty-three."

Hmm. Not what I'd thought he would say. I'd figured he'd be closer to forty. "How does a thirty-three-year-old man own his own company?"

"Good sense and fortitude." He lifted a shoulder. "Plus, I'm good at what I do."

"How did you get the money to start the company?"

"That's a conversation for another time." He slid to a stop in front of a brown-brick apartment building. "We're here."

I looked out the tinted window and up the building, then back down, taking in the street surroundings. Hip hop music blared, and a group of kids danced on the sidewalk, cheering one another on.

"What if someone recognizes me?" I wasn't sure my new brown tresses really changed my look that much. Plus, I was known for my "striking" eye color.

"You'll be fine because you're with me. They won't ask questions, and no one in this neighborhood will snitch."

I drew in a shaky breath. Right about now, I wished I could lean on God like Emmett did. What a comfort it would be to let someone else take my burdens. But I couldn't trust a God who forgave evil people. Believing in Him held no benefits for me, because I wanted revenge.

3

FOX CARRIED MY DUFFEL BAG THROUGH THE BUILDING'S TIGHT corridor. Doors lined both sides of the building's hall, but no sounds leaked through the thresholds. Obviously, this building was sturdier than I'd given it credit for. Then again, older buildings had been constructed with more quality craftmanship than today's quick-build homes. Despite our townhouse being older, we'd still paid a fortune to soundproof the rooms we needed for work purposes. Tavia was light on her feet, but no one wanted to listen to the music she blasted when practicing moves for a performance. And Holiday needed a studio that could block out the sound of her endless starts and restarts when she was in composing mode.

Me, I used a darkroom. In my spare time, I loved taking pictures. When developing them, I listened to music and imagined my cares no longer existing.

My camera! I gave myself a mental forehead slap. I'd left it behind.

Fox stopped at the door at the end of the hall and pulled a key from his pocket. Before inserting it, he turned toward me. "Listen, you have to promise not to come and go as you please. You need me to keep you safe out there and to keep questions from circling around you."

My back stiffened as I met his dark gaze. I'd always thought black eyes would be boring, but his held a steadiness that radiated strength and told me he could be trusted to do his job. And he'd been kind enough to get me away from my friends. Give them a chance to live safely and normally. The least I could do was agree without complaint.

"Okay."

"Thank you."

I simply nodded, ignoring his unspoken surprise at my easy acceptance. But truly, my acceptance wasn't so cut-and-dried. I had to fight every instinct telling me to run and not trust him. To not allow myself to be vulnerable or beholden to him. But what choice did I have? I didn't have a plan yet.

Fox entered the apartment, then waited to close the door behind me. He locked the deadbolt and entered some numbers into the security pad by the door, then the blinking red light turned green. He turned, facing the end of the apartment hall. "Grand?"

I heard a rustling noise, and then an elderly woman with a salt-and-pepper pixie cut peeked out from an opening. Her wizened face gave her an air of fragility, until she entered the hallway to walk toward us, her spine erect. She had presence. If I didn't know any better, I'd think Fox's grandmother had been someone well-known in her day.

He bent down, placing a kiss on her cheek, then wrapped her in his arms. My throat tightened at the gentleness displayed toward his petite grandmother. She had to be around five two, *maybe* five three. They pulled away from each other, and Fox gestured to me.

"Grand, this is Tori Bell. Tori, this is my grandmother, Etta Fox."

I almost jerked at his use of my nickname rather than Ms.

Bell or Princess. Then his grandmother's name grabbed my attention.

Etta? A beautiful name that suited her. "Nice to meet you, Mrs. Fox. Thank you so much for letting me stay here."

"My pleasure."

Hearing her speak only made it more difficult to guess her age. Whereas her erect bearing made her appear younger than the abundance of wrinkles suggested, the soft rasp of her voice made me wonder if she were, in fact, older.

Mrs. Fox met my gaze, her brows slightly raised. "Are you hungry?"

"A little bit."

Her eyes roved over me. "At least you're not one of those anorexic looking models."

"Oh no, ma'am. I like to eat. Just not when I'm nervous." I winced at the slip. What was it about the Foxes that made my lips loosen and spill my secrets?

A smile broke out across her face, lighting up her dark eyes—the same eyes that Fox had. She waved a hand in the air. "There's no need to be nervous. My home is your home. Make yourself comfortable."

Had I passed some kind of test? I dipped my head with a smile. "Thank you, Mrs. Fox. I really do appreciate it."

She waved her hand again and scoffed. "None of that Mrs. Fox business. My Henry passed away many years ago. It's just Etta, or you can call me *Grand*."

I could so call her by her first name. She didn't resemble the late Etta James in looks, but she had a presence about her that reminded me of the old jazz singer. "Can you sing, Miss Etta?"

She laughed, sounding like a smoker cackling. "You best believe it. Sunday is a time for blues and jazz. Not that elevator kind—no substance whatsoever—but the kind that speaks to your hurts." Her eyes looked me over. "You know the kind, don't you?"

Unfortunately. My lips flattened.

"Never mind. Let's get you fed and settled."

Fox held up my duffel. "I'll put this in the last bedroom on the left." He pointed down the hallway toward a closed door.

"Thank you."

He nodded and walked away.

I followed Miss Etta into the dining room—the one she'd popped out of a moment ago. The round table had been set, and dishes filled the center. Jerk chicken, collard greens, rice and peas (why they called it that when it was actually rice and kidney beans blew my mind, but whatever), rolls, and plantains. My stomach growled at the aromas.

"Are you Jamaican?" I asked Miss Etta.

"Our people come by that way, but I'm American, as are my grands." She motioned behind me and I whirled around, sighing when I realized it was just Fox.

"You ready to eat?" She looked up at Fox.

"Sure am, Grand."

"Sit then."

We each took a spot, and then she held out her hands. I took hers and eyed Fox's.

"I don't bite, Princess."

I swallowed down a growl and let my fingertips touch his palm.

"Let us pray," Miss Etta stated. "Dear Lord, we ask that Your hand of protection be on this child. May You give wisdom to Marcel and his crew so they may keep all their charges safe. Please come in the midst of us as we break bread and remember who You are in our lives."

"And thank you for the hands that prepared this feast," Fox interjected.

"Amen." Fox's grandmother released our hands, then clapped hers once. "Let's eat."

I looked at Fox. I didn't remember hearing his first name when my father demanded we use his services. "Marcel?"

"Fox to you."

"I don't know. I'm sure this information could be used somehow."

Fox shook his head and fixed his plate.

"Eat up, eat up." Miss Etta motioned for me to grab a plate, so I did.

The food smelled so good and reminded me of my favorite Jamaican eatery near our place in Manhattan. I hoped Holiday and Tavia would forgive me for leaving without a goodbye. Could I text them? I gasped and looked at Fox. "Should I turn my cell off?"

He shook his head. "No need. I turned it off when we were talking earlier."

I gaped at him.

"You left it on your dresser. It was a simple click of a button. I'll get you a burner tomorrow."

I wanted to lecture about invasion of privacy, but he'd done me a favor. I'd seen enough movies to know you could track a person easily through their phone.

With the first bite of the jerk chicken, an explosion of flavor coated my tongue. I couldn't help but wiggle in delight at the taste before I became conscious of my audience. Fox's expression was unreadable. The desire to shield my warming cheeks crept up on me, so I turned toward Miss Etta instead.

She wore a look of pure pleasure. Clearly, she enjoyed feeding people. Lucky for her, I could still enjoy food when not working. I wasn't like other models who put themselves on strict diets while waiting for their next job. Granted, I couldn't eat everything before me. Fast metabolism notwithstanding, I was very much aware that thirty was only three years away.

We sat eating, conversation flowing intermittently. As my stomach filled, tension seeped out of my shoulders. Maybe I really would be safe here.

A double knock sounded at the door, followed by a key

turning in the lock. I paused mid bite, staring at Miss Etta then Fox. Neither looked perturbed. Who else lived here?

"I'm home," a teenage girl's voice called.

"In here, Sasha," Miss Etta called back. She looked at me. "My great-grand."

A girl about fifteen or sixteen rounded the corner. Her milk-chocolate skin glowed with youthfulness, and her hair was a riot of gorgeous waves. Talk about hair envy.

She froze, eyes going wide as she spied my bodyguard. "Uncle Fox! You're here!"

He stood and she flew into his arms, wrapping hers around him in a death grip. "I take it you missed me, huh?" he asked with a chuckle.

I stared at the scene, mesmerized. Who *was* this man? I'd never seen him so relaxed and happy. It was a little disconcerting.

Sasha stepped out of his arms and then kissed her grandmother on the cheek. "Hey, Grand."

"Hi, sweetie. Did you have fun?"

"Oh yeah, the movie was great."

"Sasha, I'd like you to meet our house guest." Miss Etta held out a hand toward me. "Sasha, meet Tori."

Sasha smiled at me, then seemed to freeze up. Her eyes widened and her mouth parted. She pointed at me. "Is that…? That's…oh my…Ah!" She slapped her hands over her mouth, her eyes tearing up.

"Sasha?" Fox asked quietly.

She moved a hand, though it still hovered over her mouth. "Yes?"

"This is Tori. No last name. If someone asks, she's my girlfriend."

My eyes flew to him, an objection hovering over her lips. I didn't want to be *anyone's* girlfriend. But the warning he gave earlier about staying with him and letting him do his job kept me mute.

"Is she really your girlfriend?" Sasha's eyes never left mine.

Her adoration was adorable and definitely unwarranted. I was no role model.

"No, a client."

Her brow wrinkled and her eyes took on a sad puppy look. Like someone had stolen all her kibble. "Bummer."

"Sasha, you forgot to use your manners," Miss Etta scolded.

"Sorry." She drew in a big breath. "Nice to meet you. I'm a huge fan and I'll totally stay out of your way and not bug you, but can I get at least one autograph?" She exhaled, shoulders dropping with the relief of spilling her guts in one breath.

I stifled a laugh. "Nice to meet you too, Sasha. And I'd be happy to sign something."

She mouthed *oh my goodness* as she shook her hands out by her side, but then her head tilted to the side as her brow puckered. "Wait, where is she staying?"

"In your room," Miss Etta replied.

My mouth dropped. "I can't take her room."

"Oh no, you totally can. Please!" Sasha's hands gripped together in a prayer motion.

I'd have laughed if the thought of putting her out didn't horrify me.

"It'll be just fine, Tori." Miss Etta patted my hand. "She'll sleep in my room until you're taken care of."

"Are you sure?" I peered into Miss Etta's wise gaze.

"Quite. Now, Sasha, why don't you have some food? Or are you full of movie popcorn?"

"Oh no, I can eat." Sasha sat right next to me and grinned from ear to ear.

Living here would be an adventure for sure.

4

SASHA'S ROOM WAS SMALLER THAN MY CLOSET BACK AT HOME but held a hominess I'm not sure I'd ever experienced. The black wrought iron bed displayed a beautiful quilt patterned with twinkling stars, the purple-and-white arrangement seemingly perfect for a teenage girl.

I moved my duffel bag off the bed and placed it on the floor, then flopped onto my back with a sigh and stared up at the ceiling. What was I supposed to do now? How could I get this stalker to come forward so I could get back to my life? Rid myself of the 24/7 edginess that had been my constant companion since he'd started sending me creepy "presents" in the mail. Chills wracked my body.

That first note with the rose hadn't raised any red flags. It wasn't until about the third or fourth one that I'd become nervous and wondered if I had a problem. Now he was sending blatant threats and so-called gifts through the mail. That alone had earned a visit from the FBI and a collaboration with the NYPD.

Which was what had prompted my dad to hire my own personal shadow. Fox had to be everywhere I was. I tried to ignore him, but sometimes my distractions failed, and my gaze would find him standing nearby, staring. Intense scrutiny was standard issue with a security businessman's vigilant stare, wasn't it? Still didn't explain why I had a funny feeling I was off the mark. Like his staring was personal in nature.

Again with the focus on Fox! Get your head in the game and solve your stalker problem.

I groaned, rolling onto my stomach. Who was I kidding? I could no more solve the puzzle than the law enforcement officers who'd been put on my case. Everyone came up empty. Somewhere out there, a stranger roamed the streets and made plans to torture me, robbing me of my peace of mind. Or least, I hoped he was a stranger. How awful would it be if I knew my stalker?

The FBI and NYPD had made me create a list of possible suspects. Unfortunately, I'd turned down a few men who didn't understand the seriousness of my *nos* and needed to receive the message in a physical way.

So far, either everyone had an alibi or there wasn't enough evidence to deem them a plausible suspect.

Tears gathered in my eyes as I fought the onslaught of emotions. Memories of the past pushed forward, reminding me of my vulnerability against the opposite sex. The strength they often wielded as a weapon. Of the scars carved deep, changing me in ways I didn't fully understand.

Perhaps because I never wanted to examine them. They were safer in the compartment I'd placed them in. I sniffed, wiping at my face, and sat up. *You can do this. Be strong. Stay strong. Think. Plan.*

I gulped. My first line of business needed to be letting Holiday and Tavia know I was safe. They'd want to know I was okay and had left for their safety.

I stood and walked over to the oval mirror hanging over the cedar dresser. My eyes were red and my makeup streaked. Even though there were no paparazzi around to snap a picture, I grabbed my makeup bag out of the duffel to fix my face. Always looking camera ready was so ingrained in me. I had a presence to maintain. People expected me to look perfect 24/7, no matter what emotional turmoil I may be going through. Didn't matter if I wanted to walk around in pajama bottoms and a big sweatshirt while eating a bowl of ice cream.

Not to say I couldn't do those things. It's just, as soon as I stepped into a public place, I had to be *on*. Appear every inch the supermodel or risk the public's wrath. No one wanted to end up on a grocery store newsstand with rumors of a baby bump, or worse, *letting herself go*.

I shuddered. As the youngest child of the Bells—famous in their own right—I'd been taunted by the paparazzi all my life. When I was five, my face had been splashed over all the tabloids as inquiring minds speculated if I was my father's love child.

The ordeal was a grueling period for our family, and for a time, I'd believed my parents would divorce. Not because I was actually my father's illegitimate love child. Not at all. My father had never cheated on my mother, although that didn't prevent the tabloids from constantly suggesting otherwise. No, it was the incessant presence and buzz of the paparazzi in our lives that slowly chipped at my parents' marriage. They buckled under the strain, and soon words were exchanged that shouldn't have been.

I'm not honestly sure how they survived it, but they did. And ever since then, they'd ignored the tabloids and kept our home entertainment-news free. When I became independent and was thrust into that world via runways and photo shoots, I got highlighted once more. I hated how public perception had begun to dictate my reality. I had to be careful of every image I displayed on my social media accounts, the words I chose to write on any posts. I was no longer allowed to have my own opinions, because I'd become a commodity—one forced to dance and do a jig for pay. Some thought because the pay was exorbitant, I should be happy.

But when the public saw you not as a human being but as their own personal entertainment, staying in the business often became a bitter pill. If they'd spent any money to purchase a photo, a magazine, or anything with my likeness on it, then they believed they could dictate my life. Wear this. Don't do that. Don't say that.

Shut up and entertain us.

Can you recall the last time a celebrity dared voice their opinion, especially a political one? The vitriol that soon followed from their supposed *adoring* public? Their tweets and rants on social media are the proverbial crack of a whip demanding we do what they bought us for.

These thoughts followed me into sleep and invaded my dreams. Newscasters plastered my face on TV as news of my stalker broke onto mainstream media channels. Commentators and news pundits sat around questioning if my lifestyle brought on my own demise.

I woke from the dream feeling haunted. After a quick shower, I readied for the day. Today's to-do list consisted of one thing: get a burner phone.

As I left Sasha's room, I took in the sounds around me. The apartment held an odd note of quiet. I kept expecting neighboring noise to filter into the place but...nothing. In fact, it didn't even seem like Miss Etta, Sasha, or Fox were even here. My pulse beat erratically in my throat as I moved down the hall toward the living room.

Fox sat on the couch, laptop out in front of him and a Bluetooth in his ear. "Yeah, I'm going to need surveillance. Nothing conspicuous. Make sure whoever you assign blends in." He paused and looked up as I made my way toward the window seat.

He frowned and began talking again. "No. I'll be operating from here until I tell you otherwise... Yes, you can come here for report." He checked his wristwatch. "Tomorrow at eight should be fine. See you then."

I studied him from beneath my lashes under the pretense of examining the quilted pillow I'd pulled onto my lap.

"I figured you'd be resting or something."

"Too amped up." I met his gaze, trying to keep from flinching at his measured stare. "You're here early."

He shrugged, ignoring my unspoken question. "Have you come up with a plan yet?"

"No. I do know I need a phone."

He slowly nodded. "Right. I know a place down the street that sells burners."

"Can we go now?"

"Yeah." He studied me, probably noting the simple jeans and t-shirt I wore. "At least you don't scream *rich and famous* right now."

I arched an eyebrow. "Meaning I'll blend in?"

"Not a chance, Princess."

The hairs on my neck rose in irritation, but I held back. Too many times I'd wasted my energy arguing with Fox. Right now, I was very much aware that I owed him more than he owed me. Especially since he'd shielded me during that car accident.

I could still remember the warmth of his body as he cocooned me when another vehicle T-boned into us. I'd been on the hospital side of the car. How easily I could remember those horrible moments as the car slid until coming to a stop.

I shifted my thoughts. "I can add my Yankees cap."

"Fine. Get that and let's go."

I hurried to the guest room, grabbing the wallet I'd bought to replace all my name brand purses. Hopefully, it didn't scream *rich and famous* as Fox accused.

He was waiting for me in the hallway, leaning against the wall near the front door. My pulse jumped as I took in the picture he made. Steady. Dependable.

And smoldering with intensity.

I pulled up every defense I could think of to wrap around me as a fortress. The more I remembered how much of a thorn Fox was, the better my chance of coming through this whole situation unscratched.

"I'm ready."

He nodded, leading us out. "When we get to the shop, follow my lead."

I gulped. That sounded ominous. "Fine."

"You know, you're starting to make me nervous."

My eyes darted to his. "What?"

"All this 'okay' and 'fine' stuff. You're never this easy to work with, Princess."

"Maybe because you're an arrogant—"

"Ha! I knew the real you was in there somewhere."

I rolled my eyes, but more at myself than him. He'd baited me, and I'd fallen for his trap. "Let's just go get the phone."

"As you wish."

A tingle of awareness rippled through me. His whispered words did something to my insides. Softened them and made me want to lean into his strength. But I couldn't. Men weren't to be trusted. I stiffened my back and yanked on the front door, walking out with all the confidence in the world.

Okay, not really, but Fox didn't have to know that.

5

A FRESH HIP-HOP BEAT BOUNCED THROUGH THE STREETS AS WE walked down the block. My hands swung loosely by my side, and my steps fell in sync with the tempo. Too bad I was actually anything but the cool façade I presented. What if someone recognized me? Would they really keep quiet and respect my privacy just because Fox strolled next to me? Granted, he was bigger than the average male, but still. A picture of me was worth thousands of dollars. And who knew how much the stalker would pay to know my exact location? I tried not to give any facial hints at the thoughts spinning in my brain.

"Up there." Fox nodded with a jerk of his chin.

A sign advertising odds and ends hung over a small storefront.

"Remember, follow my lead."

"Should I be worried?"

"Not at all." Fox placed a hand at the small of my back and opened the door, then guided me inside.

My senses went on full alert as I stepped into the corner shop.

"Marcel, my man!" The guy behind the counter broke into

26

a wide smile as we entered. His dreads swung as he came out and back-clapped Fox. "Haven't seen you in a minute."

"Ain't that the truth. I've been...occupied." He sent an intimate smile my way and winked.

To my shame, heat bloomed in my cheeks, but my objection stuck in my throat. I had to remember that to the world watching, I was his girlfriend.

The man eyed me, and I waited for recognition to spark. "I see how it is. Your girl?"

"That she is." Fox held out a hand.

I hesitated a split second and then slid mine into his. He held my hand lightly—not that anyone watching would be able to tell—my mouth dried as the full implications hit me. Was this how he would keep me safe? Playing pretend boyfriend?

"Babe, this is Dunc. Duncan, my girl."

"Nice to meet you." I dipped my head.

"The pleasure's all mine." The dude spared me another glance and then stopped, lasering his focus on me.

Uh oh. My insides clenched as I waited for it. The recognition. That question. Then the onslaught.

His eyes widened and his gaze darted from me to Fox, but the steely look on Fox's face returned Duncan's jaw to its normal placement. "I won't say anything," he mumbled.

"Which is why I came to you instead of heading to Manny's shop." Fox pulled me to his side and wrapped an arm around my shoulders.

"A'ight. 'Preciate that, man."

"Do you?" Fox asked coolly.

"Without a doubt."

"Great." Fox dropped his arm, intertwining our fingers once more. "My lady lost her phone. Could we get one?"

"Not a problem." He paused, looking at me then back at Fox. "Burner?"

Fox simply nodded.

I hated remaining mute, but right now, that seemed the best thing to do. My focus had to be on staying safe, not inserting my pride and desire to do things my way.

That would come later.

An assortment of rings, lockets, and other jewelry items displayed in a glass case caught my eyes. Every one of those items probably had a story attached to it, but would those stories be half as bizarre as my life was beginning to feel right now?

"Need bells and whistles or just basics?"

Duncan's voice broke through my curiosity. I turned and Fox gave me a look of warning.

I bit my lip. Swallowed down disappointment. "Basics."

Oh, how I hated not being able to log on to social media, but it was best if I disappeared altogether. Already I felt the stinging loss of connection with the social world. No wonder older generations thought millennials had an addiction. In our defense, they probably felt just as antsy waiting for the postman to arrive after mailing a letter.

"Basics it is." The guy unlocked the counter display and pulled out a burner phone. "That'll be fifty bucks."

Fox pulled out his wallet and slid more than the asking price across the counter. "Keep the change. Pleasure doing business with ya."

"Anytime." He eyed me. "You need me to spread the word about ya girl?"

Concentration furrowed Fox's brow. "Not now. But if I do, you'll be the first to know."

"Bet." They slapped hands, sliding their palms across one another's, and then snapped.

There had to be a story behind their friendship—one I wanted to know. Considering I'd told Fox how Holiday and Tavia had become my besties, it was his turn to come clean. I kept silent until we were walking back to Miss Etta's home.

"Who was that?" I hooked a finger over my shoulder. "And what's up with him calling you Marcel?"

My breath hitched as Fox met my gaze. It wasn't every day that I could wear a booted heel and still have to glance up at a man. Fox made me feel small and vulnerable—two feelings I detested.

He shrugged. "You're the only one calling me Fox."

"But, Jax—"

"Nuh uh. Just you."

I pursed my lips. "And the guy?"

"We go way back."

"Thank you, Captain Obvious."

His lips twitched. "We've been friends since kindergarten. After high school, I went one path, he went another."

"Yet you seem to be on speaking terms."

"We'll be friends forever. Our paths just don't cross every day. But—" He stopped, facing me. "I trust him with my life. Which is why I went to his shop and why, when people start asking questions, I'll have him start some well-placed rumors. No one will dare contradict him."

"Then why didn't you start them now?" And what kind of rumors was he talking about? I hated insinuations. Hated what others could assume when a person was vague.

"Because you don't have a plan yet. I'm waiting to hear what you have to say before I put the rumor mill into motion. No use making a stir if you're not going to stick around."

My mouth parted and shock shuddered through me. He would just let me leave? Go off unattended?

"No, no." He held up a hand. "Your thoughts are screaming across your face."

"Really?" I had an *excellent* poker face.

He lifted a shoulder. "Is it too crazy to believe I know you better than you think?"

"Yes." Absolutely terrifying.

He smiled, and shallow dents appeared alongside his

perfectly sculpted beard. Two trim lines of hair attached his mustache to the goatee growing on his chin. And why was I noticing?

Fox took a step forward, his gaze never leaving mine. "You were wondering if I would really let you just go off by yourself unprotected." He shook his head, tsking. "Obviously, I wouldn't. I promised to protect you, and I will until…"

"Until what?"

But he didn't answer me. Simply gestured for me to continue walking. My mind mulled over his words. And darn it all if he didn't start whistling the rest of the way to Miss Etta's apartment building.

Once we got back inside, Fox helped me set up the phone, then headed for the kitchen. I sat in the recliner to make some necessary calls. Thank goodness I'd actually memorized Holiday's and Tavia's numbers. Fox had encouraged us to do so when he'd first been assigned as head of our security, saying we never knew when we'd need the info. Who knew he'd be right?

The girls probably wouldn't answer a call with an unknown number, so I'd have to leave a voicemail. However, there was another call I wanted to get out of the way first. I typed in my agent's number. McCall would be livid, but hopefully willing to put out the fires my disappearance would cause.

"McCall Inc, how may I help you?"

"Paige, this is Tori. Could you put me through to McCall?"

"Hi, Tori. I'll patch you right through."

A second later, the line clicked. "If it isn't the beautiful Bell. Are you headed to Dante's?"

I winced. How had I forgotten? "Actually, McCall…"

Her fiery voice lit the phone waves. "No, no, no. Whatever's going on, whatever you're thinking, stop."

"McCall, I need you to clear my schedule for the foreseeable future."

"No, no, no! What's going on, Tori?"

"I'm just taking a break from life."

"You can't do that when you're under contract." Indignation lit her words, and I could perfectly imagine the petite woman, her blonde waves layered to her shoulders and an e-cigarette hanging from her lips. She was a former actress turned agent—pure grit laced in steel.

"I can when my life is being threatened."

"I thought you had a bodyguard."

"I do, but didn't you hear Holiday got shot?"

"And what does that have to do with you? They were gunning for her, not you."

"I'm not sure how, but it's connected." It had to be. We couldn't both have stalkers. What were the odds?

"I'm not hearing this. You are *not* putting me in this position."

I smiled, injecting a sugary sweet tone. "That's fine. I completely understand if you have to break your association with me and end our own contract."

"Wait, that's not what I'm saying at all."

Ah, money always talked. Funny how quickly McCall could change her tune when reminded my millions brought her several thousand in income. "Are you sure? I don't want to put you in an awkward position." I may have had a tad bit of perverse pleasure repeating her phrase.

"And you won't be. Your safety is paramount."

Interesting how she came to that conclusion *after* I'd threatened to walk. Nevertheless, she was doing me a huge favor. "Thank you, McCall."

"Call me when you can."

"Will do." I hung up and sighed.

At least that was done. I dialed Emmett next, but no answer. Now to call Holiday and Octavia. Was there any chance they were together and I could kill two birds with one stone?

I winced at the analogy. Not a good one to use.

I tapped in Holiday's number first. The line rang and rang until, finally, the voicemail clicked on.

Not that I'd expected her to answer. Still, I hung up after letting her know I was safe, then dialed Tavia's number. Maybe she would answer and if luck won out, they would be together. After two rings, her voice called out in greeting. Trust her to pick up.

"It's Tori."

"Tori! We've been looking everywhere for you. We were supposed to go to brunch."

Oh no. I'd forgotten today was our standing date. "Did you go?"

"No. You know if one of us is missing, we skip."

I smiled. I loved our Sunday brunch outings. "I'm sorry I missed it. It totally slipped my mind."

"Then you're good? You're okay?"

"I…" I could do this. Admit that I was nowhere they could find me. "I'm taking a break, Tavia."

"What does that mean?"

"What did she say?"

I chuckled as I heard Holiday's question in the background. "Just put me on speaker."

"All right."

"Tori, where are you?" Holiday asked in her no-nonsense tone.

"I decided to get away, take the danger from you two, so don't try and find me."

"You what?!" Holiday shouted. Tavia uttered some exasperation in Italian.

"Do you *not* remember what happened to Emmett?" I fought the tears as a picture of my brother wounded and lying in a hospital bed came to mind. "He was shot, Hol."

"Yes, but the police said I was the target. It had nothing to do with you."

"Can you guarantee that?"

Silence filled the phone.

"It doesn't matter if she can or not," Tavia spoke up. "What matters is your safety. Come home so the security team can watch over you."

"I'm with Fox." I held my breath, waiting for their recriminations.

"I knew it!"

I could practically see Holiday dancing. I should have FaceTimed them, but I didn't want to give my location away. "There's nothing to know."

"Uh huh. Sure there's not," Holiday said in a singsong voice.

And dang it if her patronizing tone didn't sound as musical as her songs on the radio. Did every word out of her mouth have to sound golden?

"I think you guys would make a good couple," Tavia offered.

"I'm *not* in the market for a boyfriend."

"I seem to recall saying something similar," Holiday said. "And you told me that I needed to give Emmett a chance. Maybe you should give Captain Yumminess a chance."

"Captain what?" My lips parted.

Tavia giggled.

"Oh, right. My mistake. I've been trying to forget the nicknames."

"Wait. Does everyone have one?"

"Just him and Jax. I was reformed by the time Ty and the others came on board."

"So, what's Jax's?" I was curious about the man who could be a double for Chris Hemsworth, or at least his brother.

"Hottie McCutie," Holiday said in a tone reminiscent of a child about to get in trouble.

I fell back against the living room recliner, guffaws erupting from me.

"Does Emmett know?" Tavia asked.

"It hasn't come up."

"Well, Fox is definitely yummy-looking as long as he doesn't talk."

Holiday snorted and Tavia murmured in agreement.

I was really going to miss seeing them.

Fox walked into the room, amusement quirking the corner of his lips. "Hey, ladies, I have to go."

Had he heard our conversation? The nicknames? My comment? Heat pooled in my face.

"You promise Fox is there?"

I pressed the speaker button and motioned for Fox. "Fox, say something so Tavia and Holiday believe I haven't left all forms of security."

"Ms. Brown, Ms. Ricci, I'll watch her back."

"Thank you," they chorused.

I hung up and looked over my shoulder at Fox.

"I knew you liked me." He winked.

❧ 6 ❧

THE NEXT MORNING, I AWOKE TO GRITTY EYES AND THE STAIN OF every nightmare that had plagued my sleep. Replays of Emmett taking a bullet, blood seeping from his chest. Images of Holiday and Tavia tied up and gagged. The searing pain of a bullet driving through my heart. My pulse drummed in my ears as sweat slid down my spine.

My body ached and I felt as strung out as an addict. Two days of bad dreams were enough to make me avoid sleep in the future. I could only hope a hot shower would erase the phantoms clinging to the recesses of my mind and make me halfway human.

When I emerged a half hour later, I felt more alert and less sore.

Coffee. I needed caffeine to jump start my system. Being in another person's home was strange and left me feeling awkward. I didn't want to disturb anyone and couldn't tell if Miss Etta and Sasha were awake or still asleep.

My ever-present shadow would be awake already. He'd shocked me last night by informing me he'd be sleeping on the sofa. I'd offered Sasha's room, but he just looked at me as if I wasn't the brightest crayon for asking that question.

If luck prevailed, he'd have started the coffee, yet I couldn't smell anything brewing. I snuck into the kitchen and my heart fell to my toes.

No Miss Etta. No Fox. No Sasha. Almost a repeat from yesterday. A glance in the dining room proved that to be empty as well. I moved across the hall and peeked in the living room. A fissure of relief unlocked the tension that had been building in my shoulders. Fox sat on the sofa, hunched over a newspaper laid out on the coffee table. As if this were a perfectly normal day.

"Morning."

I didn't bother being surprised that he could sense my presence without even looking up. He'd been doing that to me since he'd taken the bodyguard position. "Morning. Miss Etta still asleep?"

He lifted his head and met my gaze. "Not at all. Probably out at the market gathering fresh fruit for breakfast."

My stomach rumbled at the thought of food. Thank goodness I wouldn't starve. I'd never bothered learning to cook and depended on other people's skill. I had no shame and enjoyed every meal.

Fox motioned toward two Starbucks coffee cups on the coffee table. "Thought you'd need fortification."

"Oh, thank you." I swiftly crossed the room and snagged the offered cup. "What did you get me?"

"Hazelnut bianco latte. Your usual."

Mm. A leisurely sniff sent endorphins through my system. Tavia usually made coffee at our place, but I always preferred this bliss in a cup. "Thank you."

I took a sip and closed my eyes with pleasure. My lips curved upward as my taste buds swooned in delight. Another sip and I'd be on my way toward being a decent human to do life with. I sank into the nearby brown leather recliner, peering at Fox in between sips.

"Do you have something to ask, or are you just going to keep giving my skin the heebie jeebies?"

A sputtered laugh fell from my lips. "The heebie jeebies?"

"Come on, like you've never experienced that creepy crawly sensation when someone's eyeing you." He met my gaze, skepticism tingeing his.

"Sure, but I'd never call it the heebie jeebies." Just saying the phrase made my lips twitch. Hearing a six-foot-three bodyguard use the term made me want to press a pillow to my face to stifle my laughter. I let out a shaky breath and the suppressed chuckles along with it.

"And why not?"

"That's how kids talk."

"Whatever. That's real."

I chuckled, shaking my head. Amusement tickled my insides, but the shadows of last night kept me from succumbing. I sighed. "What am I going to do, Fox?"

"No plan yet?"

I shook my head.

"I may have one. Want to hear it?"

Shrugging, I met his steady gaze. As much as Fox's constant presence chafed, I couldn't ignore the strength I drew from him. He'd unknowingly kept me from falling apart. Whenever I wanted to cave into the stress of the situation, knowing he was there, seeing the control in his eyes, bolstered me. No one had a clue how close I was to giving in to hysteria.

"Go for it." I folded my legs and tucked my feet to the right, sinking deeper into the recliner cushions.

He leaned forward, his fingers steepled. "You keep your work engagements. You even ramp up the events you attend. But when the day is over, you come back here, safe and out of sight." He paused as if searching for words. "And I step out of the shadows as a mere bodyguard and stand by your side as your fiancé."

What the what!

My breath came in spurts at the absurdity of his plan. "That will never work!"

"Why not?" His dark eyes pierced me.

Because… "I've never been linked to anyone romantically." Yeah, let's go with that option and not the one making my pulse skitter. I needed to ignore exactly how much I was aware of him.

"Which will make this even more believable. You've never been accused of a publicity stunt or had your name attached to a long list of leading men. And people will totally buy the bodyguard romance."

Ugh. I hated how rabid bats erupted in my stomach at his use of the word *romance.* I didn't *want* a relationship, and despite the heckling my roomies gave me, certainly didn't want one with Fox. Even if I couldn't completely ignore the attraction simmering under the surface, I sure planned on denying it.

I needed to fall back on logic. "How is having a fiancé supposed to save me anyway?"

"I've reread every note, card, and letter your stalker sent. Looked through the 'gifts.'" He grimaced. "This guy, whoever he is, thinks you belong to him. If you show him you're with someone else, it'll draw him out, and we'll be able to catch him."

Fox wanted to use me as bait? I gulped. "You'll catch him before he gets me?" Because no way did I want my nightmares from last night to become reality.

"I promise you I will protect you with my last breath."

Heat flushed through me at his declaration. I knew it wasn't one of love, but my body almost swooned as if he'd used those three words instead. I looked down at my coffee lid. McCall would be ticked if I resumed my schedule after asking her to clear it. Then again, once she found out I was increasing my event commitments, she'd be elated.

But could I do this? Walk around Manhattan as if I were in love? I'd never been in love. *Never*.

"I don't know," I murmured, meeting Fox's gaze once more.

"Think about it. You don't have to make a decision today, but the sooner you do, the quicker this could all end."

I nodded, feeling like a bobble head. My anxiety couldn't seem to rein in the nervous motion. I purposely took another sip of coffee to regain the cool façade I'd perfected. If we were going to pretend to be engaged, my PR firm would need to release a statement. Or I could simply go the social media route.

"How could you pretend to be in love with me?" My eyes widened when I realized the question rolling in my mind had been spoken out loud. I'd wanted to mull it over some more before asking—or deciding I didn't want the answer.

Fox opened his mouth—

The deadbolt to the front door unlatched and the alarm beeped. "Breakfast is here," Miss Etta called out.

Fox rose to his feet, and I watched as he assisted her. Relief came quickly, almost as welcome as my latte. I could escape the awkwardness of my question until Fox brought it back up. And he would. That was how he worked.

I escaped to Sasha's room and grabbed the burner phone off the dresser, then dialed Tavia's number. Holiday might still be sleeping, but Tavia woke before the sun to work on her dance regimen.

"Tor, you okay?" Tavia's breathless voice answered.

"Yes. I'm fine. I have a dilemma and need some advice stat."

"Hold on and I'll find Holiday."

I listened to the background noises. Sounded like Tavia was using our intercom system to locate our other roommate.

"She's coming."

"Thanks, Tavia."

"Of course." A minute passed. "She's here. You're on speaker."

I quickly told them Fox's plan.

"Oh…" Holiday drew out. "Please pick this option so I can have a front seat to your fall."

"What?" I stared at the phone in confusion. She wanted to see me hurt?

Tavia chuckled. "She's practically foaming at the mouth over here, Tori."

"I don't get it. You *want* me to be bait?"

"Oh, sweetie, no. Not in a million years. But you and Fox posing as engaged has comedy gold written all over it. Y'all can't even be in the same room without sparks flying around."

I snorted. "I've mellowed."

"Yeah, because you're not in your own environment. Come back home and the sparks will resume."

"She's right, Tori." Tavia cut in. "I'm always tempted to use the fire hydrant on you two."

Holiday laughed. "It's funny 'cuz it's true!"

Tavia giggled.

"I can't believe you two. Acting like teenagers when I'm trying to fight off a stalker."

Silence descended. I winced. Maybe I had been too harsh. They meant no harm. For goodness' sake, I'd been teasing Holiday about Emmett not so long ago.

"I'm so sorry," Holiday said. "I meant no offense. Just giving you a little bit of what you gave me with Emmett."

Ugh. Pile the guilt higher. "You're right. I'm just a little…"

"Anxious?" Tavia supplied. "We know. But if Fox thinks this could work, then don't you think you should try?"

"You did take all those acting classes, Tor," Holiday added.

"True. But he hasn't."

"Come on, security has to know how to blend in and what not. I'm sure he can look the part."

My eyes widened. That was it. If I could make Fox look the part—the part Hollywood and the rest of the world expected to see—then people really might buy it. "Holiday, you're a genius."

"Duh."

I rolled my eyes. "I'm going to go find Fox. I'll update ya later."

"Bye," they chimed.

❦ 7 ❧

I HANDED FOX A WET PLATE. AFTER BREAKFAST, WE'D BOTH offered to wash the dishes, so Miss Etta put us to work. She was currently relaxing in front of the TV watching talk shows while I washed and Fox dried.

For the past few minutes, the only sounds filling the kitchen had been the running water and dishes clanking together as Fox put them in the cabinets. I should probably break the silence, but thinking about being his fiancé seemed to have rendered me mute.

"I called your father and gave him an update."

I winced. "The fiancé update, or just I'm staying with your grandmother and hiding?"

"The latter."

"Okay." I exhaled as I rinsed the cup.

"Cat got your tongue?"

I startled at the amusement in Fox's voice. I'd totally been sucked in by my thoughts. "Maybe."

"I take it you're giving my idea some serious thought? I fully expected you to laugh for a good half hour."

My lips quirked. If pretending to get close to him didn't terrify me so much, I would have totally laughed.

"But this quiet contemplation, I have to say, is getting under my skin."

My hands froze, and the spoon I held fell directly under the water running from the faucet. Time slowed as the stream of water deflected, hitting Fox square in the face. He sputtered, waving his hands in front of his nose. I quickly shut off the water.

"Oh no! I'm *so* sorry. That was a complete accident."

He dragged a towel down his face, then pierced me with his dark eyes. A mischievous glint sparked, and my stomach dropped to my toes.

"I promise it was an accident." The words rushed out as I took a backward step. "That was *not* intentional. I'm not trying to—"

I squealed as Fox scooped up a palm full of dirty dish water and flung it at me. I leaped back, but it was too late. The water dripped down my face, and my wet hair clung to my head. We stared at one another for a beat before I spoke, my voice deadly quiet. "Oh, it's like that, huh?"

Fox took a step back. I grabbed a plate from the bottom of the sink and flung the water with all my might. *Splash.* I froze, realizing my mistake. If I wanted to dart around him, there was now a chance I would slip on the wet floor. I looked up as Fox lurched for the spray nozzle, aiming it at me.

My hands shot upward. "I surrender."

"Do you now?" He tilted his head, squinting an eye. "All I have to do is turn that faucet on and you're toast."

"But you wouldn't do that. Would you?" I gestured to my wet clothing. "I'm already wet."

"Which is why a little extra won't hurt."

"But Fox," I whined. "You got my hair wet."

He shook his head. "Black women and their hair."

He'd understand if he realized how many hours went into keeping our locks under control. Having short hair didn't make the process more palatable. I could practically feel mine curling up. He put the nozzle back in place, and I breathed out a sigh of relief.

"Don't move. I need to mop this up before one of us wipes out."

"I walk on runways for a living. Pretty sure it's gonna be you, pal."

He smirked and walked out of the kitchen. A few seconds later, he returned with a mop. I bit back laughter at the mop handle that barely reached his waist.

"A little small for you, huh?"

"I have appropriately sized cleaning tools at my own place."

My eyes flew to his. "Your place?"

"Mm hm. Want to see it, do ya?" He arched an eyebrow.

"Of course not." I so did. What did he look like in his own element? Still commanding, or relaxed and unguarded? "Where do you live?"

He snorted. "None of your business, Princess."

"Whatever." I stomped past him, but he called for me just as I reached the doorway. "Yes?"

"Are you in?"

I could pretend I didn't know what he was talking about, but that would be foolish. Precious time was wasting. "Yes."

I heard his audible sigh. "Then we need to talk."

"After I save my hair."

He chuckled. "Come get me when you're done. We'll go to your room."

I whirled around. "Why?"

"To...talk." He spoke slowly and deliberately, like he was talking to a two-year old.

"Oh." I flushed. But did we have to do it in a bedroom, alone? "What about the living room?"

"Grand's watching her shows."

"Dining room?"

"Do you want her overhearing?"

"Fine," I growled. I stalked to Sasha's room and rushed to the dresser mirror.

My hair had started to frizz, losing the sleek look fast. If he'd sprayed me with more water, my whole head would have curled. Instead, my hair wavered in that halfway state that made me seem unkempt. I quickly went to work righting my appearance. Once I'd finished, I changed into a dry shirt and jeans and then went back to the kitchen.

"You ready?"

I nodded and went back to my temporary room. I could do this. Plan our fake engagement like nothing affected me. *You got this, Tori.*

Goosebumps raced up my arms as Fox sat down at the edge of the bed. I scooted closer to the headboard. *Don't be nervous. This is Fox.* But my internal pep talk fell on deaf ears. I *was* nervous. Being alone with a man brought me nothing but disaster.

Fortunately, he left the door open midway, allowing anyone to easily peek in.

"Are you not worried someone will hear us?" I motioned toward the door.

"Sasha went to school, and Grand should have the TV loud enough to drown out any noise in here."

My heart stopped, then picked up double time. I fought to suck in a breath.

Fox studied me. "Are you okay?"

"Sure." I just needed oxygen. *Think of something else.* "Where are Sasha's parents?"

Fox grimaced. "My sister passed away a couple of years ago, and her father's a deadbeat."

I winced. Such a tragic thing to happen to someone so sweet. "Do you have custody of her?"

"Joint guardianship with my grandmother. Candace asked for us to both raise her, which works out well when my job takes me out of the city or even out of state."

I nodded. Fox would make the perfect guardian. It would be amusing to see his reaction when Sasha started dating. I opened my mouth to say something, but he interrupted.

"You don't have to go through with the engagement, you know. We can come up with another idea." His voice held a note of caution and ease that surprised me.

"You think there's a better option?"

"No, but if you can't fake that happy feeling, no point in going forward. He has to believe we're in love."

My stomach dipped. "I did some acting in high school."

"Were you any good?"

I stared at him, letting my facial expression speak for me.

"Okay then. So, we're good?"

"I don't know. Can *you* act?"

"Of course I can, Princess. You think I like even half my clients?"

I shook my head wordlessly, trying not to laugh and then wondering if I was one of those.

"Well, they don't know that, and I get repeat service."

"Which clients are we talking about exactly?"

Fox smiled like an evil genius from a kids' cartoon show.

I shook my head. "What's the plan?"

"We go back to Dunc's store and see if he has an engagement ring he can loan me. I take a picture of it on your manicured hand, and you post it to all your social media."

"Oh no. I have the publicity side covered. I need to know your plan for keeping me safe."

He jerked back. "What do you mean, publicity side?"

"My name does have some pull around the city, you know. We can get into pretty much any jeweler, and they'll happily offer us the use of a ring. A supermodel can't exactly walk around with pawn shop goods."

"I can't afford—"

I held up a hand. "But *I* can. If I can't for some reason, I'm sure my father will."

Fox swallowed, the first hint of nerves peeking through. I wasn't ashamed of how happy that made me.

"Fine."

"Also, we'll need to get you some suits."

"I own two already."

"And I'll get you better ones." I gave him a look that dared him to argue. "If you're going to accompany me to events, you need to look the part."

He ran a hand over his chin. "How do you stand this?"

"It's all I know." But he was right. There were so many moments where I couldn't stand the magnifying glass. The invisible yardstick they constantly measured me against.

But I was a chameleon, fully able to adapt and change as the situation dictated. That was how I had survived so long in an industry that willingly chewed up their subjects and spat out the particles for all to see. "The security plan?"

"I'll call in favors to ensure I have the best people at every event we attend. I'll also get a mini GPS tracker to add to your watch or one of the accessories you wear every day."

I held up my left hand, wiggling my ring finger. "If the diamond's big enough, we can get it added."

"Good idea."

I looked at Fox, taking in his steady gaze. "Then we're doing this?"

He dropped to one knee and smirked. "Will you be my pretend fiancée so I can catch your stalker?"

I exhaled. "Yes."

❧ 8 ❧

MILLIONS OF WOMEN DREAMED OF RECEIVING A FAMOUS BLUE BOX —well, more aqua in my opinion—and I couldn't think of a better place to get an engagement ring. After telling McCall to resume my schedule and add some events, I made a call to the jewelry store manager at Tiffany's. She'd outfitted me with jewels for every major red-carpet occasion I'd attended in the city. No use breaking tradition for my fake engagement ring.

An employee answered the phone after two rings, and I asked to speak to the manager. After identifying myself, she put me right through.

"Tori, darling, how can I help you today?"

"Hey, Beth, I need a huge favor."

"Certainly. Tell me what it is, and I'll make it happen."

"My boyfriend just proposed—"

"Boyfriend!" Her epic squeal completely shattered my right eardrum.

I switched my cell to the other side, wincing at the ringing in my ear.

"I didn't know you were dating anyone!"

"Beth, you know I don't put my private life out there."

"True, true. And you need a ring?"

"He's a little nervous picking one out on his own, but I told him you'd love to help us."

"Oh, darling, you were absolutely correct. Don't you know when you get engaged with one of our rings, you'll be married forever?"

I blanched, grateful she couldn't see me through the phone. *It's pretend. Just pretend.*

"When can you come by?"

"Tomorrow?" We needed to get Fox a new wardrobe today.

"Oh perfect. How's ten? We'll make a show of it."

"Perfect." Just what I needed in our little publicity stunt.

The next call was to one of my designer friends. His clothes were trending in the male market, and my followers would easily be able to tell where Fox shopped for his clothes. Luc would happily supply everyday wear as well as the evening look required in the city. Thankfully, he was willing to squeeze us into his afternoon schedule. I ended the call and went searching for Fox.

Sasha paused in front of Grand's door, her eyes going wide as I entered the hallway.

"How was school, Sasha?"

Her mouth opened. Closed. Opened once more.

"Was it a good day?"

Her head moved up and down so fast I was worried she would give herself whiplash.

"Have you seen Fox?"

She pointed down the hall, her face twitching as if attempting a smile but too caught up in a fangirl moment to pull one off. I smiled and thanked her. I hoped she would warm up to me and come to realize I was just an average girl.

Okay, yeah, even I had to admit that sounded a little pretentious. I couldn't deny my fame any more than I could the color of my skin.

I found Fox in the dining room, pounding away on his laptop. The sound of Miss Etta watching TV in the next room seemed abnormally loud. Was she losing her hearing?

I shook my head and refocused. "Hey, Fox. You have a clothes fitting in an hour."

His head jerked up, mouth dropping open.

I arched an eyebrow, waiting for his response.

"Fine." He looked back down at his screen, shaking his head and muttering under his breath.

I stifled the urge to laugh. About time someone else was off-center. "Fox?" I slid into the chair across from him.

"Yes?"

"We need to come up with a story." He looked confused, so I continued. "You know, how we met? How you proposed, etcetera?" My hands moved as I talked, punctuating my sentences. Truthfully, I was too nervous to keep still.

"I've been giving it some thought." He leaned to the side, draping his arm across the back of the chair. "I met you when I became your bodyguard this June."

"Okay, that makes sense."

"Stick as close to the truth as possible, and it's a lot harder to get trapped in a lie."

What was that supposed to mean? Did he lie often? The hairs on the back of my neck prickled.

"Look, Princess, sometimes you have to distort the truth to keep yourself and others alive. Understand?"

"Isn't that wrong?" And since when did I have such a strict moral code?

"There are instances when I think lying is easier to forgive than others."

"For instance?"

"Like when Rahab lied about having the Hebrew spies in her home so that she could save them from the degenerates who lived in her town. As a result of her lie, they were protected, and Rahab earned a spot in Jesus' lineage."

I gaped at him. "Are you a *Christian?*"

He arched an eyebrow. "Why do you say it like that?"

"I'm…it's just that…" *Hmm.* I couldn't really think of anything to explain the flustered feelings heating my cheeks. I shrugged.

"Is that a problem for you?"

"No. Emmett's a Christian." And I thought Holiday had converted as well, but wasn't completely positive. Her interest in going to church had certainly been piqued though.

"But you were shocked I could be one?"

"More like…surprised by the unexpected." I hadn't pegged Fox as someone willing to let injustice go unanswered. He was, after all, trying to stop someone from hurting me. If my stalker did end up hurting me—I shuddered—would Fox's belief allow him to forgive as if nothing traumatic had happen to me?

He cocked his head. "Maybe this is a conversation for another day?"

Tension drained from my body and I nodded.

"As for how I popped the question, that's simple."

"It is?"

"I introduced you to my grandmother, and after she told me you were a keeper, I had to propose. Not every day a woman meets Grand's approval."

My cheeks flamed even hotter, and a little portion—okay, a whole lot—of me wanted that to be true. Keeping my poker face intact, I nodded. "Okay."

"Anything else we should know about each other?"

"Birthdays?"

He nodded. "I'll be thirty-four on October tenth."

"Oh, that's next month. I'll be twenty-eight, November eighth."

"Then maybe we should plan the wedding for December." He winked.

Holy Hannah! My heart took an exhilarating dive at his

wink, and for a moment, just a moment, I basked in the attraction that bloomed in me. The deep grooves in his face made an appearance. Grooves too long to be dimples but with the same impact. I wanted to place my hands on my own cheeks, but that would be telling.

Back to business, Tori. I rose to my feet and peeked at my watch. "Should we head out?"

"Yeah, sounds good." He looked at my outfit. "Are you able to go back out in the world like that?" He motioned to my yoga pants and loose-fitting T-shirt.

I shrugged. "Eh, I can today. Luc's place is secure, and no one will see us going in or leaving. Tomorrow, I'll be social media ready."

"Fair enough."

We drove to Luc's in silence except for the random directions I gave. For the most part, my mind was too busy worrying about how I was going to pretend to be *in love*. I needed to remember every single acting class and lessons my parents had taught me about how to present myself in front of others and project the image I wanted them to see. It was time to put on a public persona that was also an in-love persona.

Fox stopped in front of the iron gate that led to Luc's warehouse. "Now what?"

I held up my phone, already dialing Luc's number. "*Oui, ma belle*, you are here?"

"Yes, Luc. We just pulled up in a black Escalade."

"*Très bien*, pull through."

The iron gate opened, and I motioned for Fox to drive forward.

"You know the way, ma belle."

"Yes. See you in a sec, Luc."

Fox stopped the car, and I turned around, my heart suddenly in my throat as I scanned our surroundings.

"Relax. I'm just waiting until the gate closes once more. I want to make sure no one sneaks in with us."

"Thank you." I sank into the leather cushion. I would have never thought of that.

"I'll always do my job."

"I know." And maybe that would be enough for me to fake an in-love impression.

Shouldn't be that hard to show gratitude to the man who kept me alive. I just needed to figure out a way to transfer that feeling to a façade the public would believe.

I directed Fox to the back entrance, where we could exit under a covered walkway and immediately enter the warehouse without fear of anyone watching. Luc's security guard was already waiting for us. He gave me a nod and opened the door.

"Thank you."

"My pleasure, Ms. Bell."

I walked down the covered walkway and entered the never-ending hall that led to Luc's workspace. Finally, the room opened to an industrial area. A showstopping display of windows allowed a magnificent array of light to pour in. Designer tables cluttered the area with clothing racks mixed into the scene. Luc's personal space was one of the tables in here somewhere. He couldn't bear to be too far away from the action, although I knew he had an office on the upper floor.

"Ma belle!" Luc held out his hands as he ambled toward us. He stopped right in front of me and leaned forward to kiss me on my right cheek then the left. His finger pointed accusingly at my clothes. "What are you wearing? This is not *Juste Luc.*"

"Of course not. I was doing some...cleaning, so I threw these on."

He nodded, a flop of dark hair falling across his brow. He flung his head back, his dark eyes assessing me, then he abruptly pivoted, looking Fox in the face as he held out a hand. "I am Luc."

"Marcel Fox, Tori's fiancé."

I raised an eyebrow at the extra bass in Fox's voice.

"Your…fiancé?" Luc blinked at us, his smile freezing for a moment before stretching even wider. "Well, this is a surprise!" He clapped his hands together. "Such a surprise. You have been holding out on me, *méchante fille*." He wiggled an admonishing finger at me before assessing Fox with his frank gaze. His face puckered in a frown. "Bien. You will need a new wardrobe, *non*?"

Fox glanced at me, a slight panic in his eyes. I glided up to him, sliding my hand up his back. "Please help us, Luc. I have some events coming up and Fox needs to dress accordingly."

"Ah." He shrugged and gave Fox a knowing look. "They always try and change us, do they not?"

Fox chuckled. "Always."

"Oh, but I don't want to change him." I peered up at Fox, batting my eyelashes just a bit. "He's perfect the way he is." I waited a beat before facing Luc. "I just need the clothes to showcase what I already know."

"*Mais oui*, of course." He clapped his hands. "How would you describe your fiancé?"

"Honorable, dependable, and protective."

Luc nodded, rocking his chin on his pointer fingers. He appeared moody, eyes rimmed with black eyeliner. The dark lines matched the ink going up and down his arms and the dark hair that hinted at his bad-boy appeal.

"*Vraiment*, I know the perfect ensemble. I will be right back." He snapped his fingers in the air. "Vicky, come!"

The blonde who had been quietly stitching at a table scurried after him.

I stepped away from Fox.

"Not what I expected."

"What? Luc or the whole ordeal?" I gestured around us.

"All of it. His personality, the warehouse, the fact that he gave me the stink eye as if I'd stolen his prized possession."

I laughed in bemusement. "Luc doesn't like me like that."

"Such a woman!" Fox shook his head. "He's into you. Probably why he was giving his clothes away for free."

"I'm a model. I get a lot of free clothes."

"Have you ever paid for some?"

"Sure."

"From Luc?"

My stomach tensed. "No."

"He likes you. I just hope he doesn't hate me enough to put me in something ridiculous."

"He wouldn't. You're going to go out and say you're wearing his designs. It would be a career killer to make you look anything but spectacular." And part of me was giddy with anticipation. What would Fox look like in a tux?

Pretend, Tori, pretend.

"But I bet I'll be getting a bill."

"It'll go on my expense account." I turned away.

Fox was being ridiculous. Luc was simply a friend. Besides, I would never date someone I did business with. Present circumstances excluded, of course.

A few hours later, we left with some suits, an overcoat, jeans that made Fox look a little too yummy, and various other items. Luc even gifted me an outfit to wear to the jeweler's the next day.

As we drove away, I couldn't help but wish for a pause button. Nevertheless, tomorrow's craziness was going to happen whether I was ready or not.

❧ 9 ❧

MY FIVE-FOOT-TEN REFLECTION FILLED THE FLOOR-LENGTH mirror. The red lace dress I wore was pure perfection. It brought out the warm tones in my coloring, making my brown skin glow with vitality. The cap-length flutter sleeves flirted with the tops of my arms, and the dress fell just above my knees. My gold Saint Laurent heels complemented the vision.

I was proposal ready—complete with a simple French manicure to help me show off whatever ring we'd choose.

I walked out of Sasha's room and came to a halt.

Fox leaned against the hall wall, legs covered in dark washed jeans and crossed at the ankles. He wore a pale gray button-up shirt, the sleeves rolled high enough to see the muscles in his forearms. My mouth went dry.

He straightened, and a look of admiration flashed so quickly on his face I almost missed it.

Almost.

"You ready, Princess?"

"We shall see."

He held out his hand. "Then let's get this show started."

"Right." I slid my hand in his, barely stifling the gasp that

56

wanted to erupt at the warmth of his touch. Something about the heat begged me to curl my hand tighter around his. But I stayed strong and kept my hand loose, fighting the impulse to draw closer to him.

Thankfully, the hand holding stopped once we got in the car. Before I could ready my mind for upcoming events, Fox had pulled up in front of the store. A valet opened my door before going to the other side to retrieve the keys from Fox. After handing them over, Fox joined me on the sidewalk and took my hand while scanning the area, ever vigilant.

Low lighting gave the building's interior an intimate atmosphere. A few patrons glanced our way when we walked in. One set of eyes widened in recognition. My stomach tightened. Would they break the news before we could? An employee quickly approached with a welcoming smile.

So it begins.

I pulled in a breath and smiled my cover-model smile. "We have a ten o'clock appointment with Beth."

The brunette blinked and gave a simple nod. "Yes, she's expecting you, Ms. Bell."

She led us to a long glass-case counter in the back, and Beth made an immediate appearance. She came around the counter and gave me a hug. "Oh, I'm so happy for you." She shook Fox's hand. "I'm Beth."

"Marcel Fox."

"Congratulations, Mr. Fox. You've got yourself a winner."

"That I do." He smiled down at me intimately, and warmth crept up my cheeks.

Instead of pushing the blush away, I let it do its thing. The added hue would give the impression I was wildly happy rather than overly anxious.

"Aw, so romantic." Beth clasped her hands together and beamed, looking at the both of us. "Now, Mr. Fox, do you have an idea of what you'd like to see Tori in?"

His eyes perused my face, as if thinking, assessing me.

Those steady eyes seemed to have an extra spark of fire today. That or I was totally misreading and imagining…what? Did I *want* him to be attracted?

"I was thinking something pear shaped would look beautiful on her."

I stifled my shock. How did he even know the different shapes engagement rings came in?

Beth nodded enthusiastically. "Absolutely." She quickly unlocked the display case and pulled out a few engagement rings, placing them artfully and with care on a velvet cushion waiting on the glass display case.

I had to admit, I was a little lightheaded at the thought of wearing an engagement ring out of the store. Wearing one on my left-hand ring finger was loads different than sporting something sparkly on my right hand to be admired at a red-carpet event. Even if this was just pretend, the world would believe I'd found my ever-after. Could I really go through with this?

Beth pointed to the first ring. "This comes with a wedding band studded with diamonds. It would be a great set for her."

Fox shook his head, and Beth pointed to the next option, clearly believing Fox was in charge. I had come in with the intent of looking at princess-cut diamonds, but I couldn't help but feel slightly giddy at the beautiful rings before me. Maybe pear-shaped *was* the way to go.

You're never getting married, remember? It wasn't in my plans. I was too damaged from being treated as a commodity. And too jaded to believe the world had more good men than bad.

"This one is flanked by two pink morganites." Beth's voice startled me, and I refocused, hoping I appeared interested.

"No, those look like they'll stab someone."

I stifled my laugh, but Beth gave a nervous chuckle. "Okay. Nothing dangerous for your lady love." She pointed to the third and final ring. "What do you think of this one, Mr. Fox?"

"May I?"

"Please."

He picked up the last ring, slowly turning it left and right as if searching for a flaw.

"That's our aquamarine set. Isn't it lovely?" Beth clasped her hands together, clearly feeling romantic and wistful. "The halo effect of the clustered diamonds really gives the jewel a cool-blue look instead of a deep one."

"Yes," he murmured. He gave Beth a brief nod and then pierced me with his gaze. Before I could ask what was wrong, he dropped to one knee. "Tori Bell, you have bewitched me, body and soul, and I never wish to be parted from you. Will you marry me?"

I stared in shock as he quoted from one of my favorite movies of all time. He hadn't said he loved me or asked if my feelings had changed, but the Darcy declaration was like a gut punch and I gasped. A slight sound, but audible to those around me. I swallowed, remembering this was for show and I needed to respond.

"Yes," I breathed.

Fox's eyes closed in relief and then opened, a jubilant grin covering his face. He slid the ring onto my finger and then rose, gathering me into his arms. I buried my face in his chest, embarrassed by the clapping going on in the background. *Just pretend. Just pretend.*

"Perfect!" Beth exclaimed.

I pulled away and looked at my friend. "What's perfect?"

She waved a black cell phone in the air. "I got it all on video just like your fiancé requested."

"You did what now?" I looked at Fox. Hadn't I told him I had the publicity side covered?

"Surprise." He leaned down and whispered in my ear. "I understand how publicity works too, Princess."

I pinched his side and moved away as he chuckled. *Infuriating man!*

Beth shook her head as if he got me good. I forced myself to ignore the irritation simmering in my insides. Why did he have to handle me? We were supposed to be in this together. He was security and I was the face. A perfect combination.

Nevertheless, a video would garner more attention than a picture of my ring finger. Now I could do both.

We quickly signed the necessary paperwork to leave with the stunning bridal set in our possession—well, mine anyway.

"It was a pleasure doing business," Beth said, shaking Fox's hand then mine.

"We appreciate you squeezing us in so soon. I can't thank you enough, Beth."

"Anytime. You know how much I love helping you, Tori. And whenever you're ready, we'll post the video on our social media pages and tag you in them. Is that good?" Beth looked at Fox, who looked at me.

"That sounds wonderful. Could you post it in half an hour? I plan on making my own announcement in a few minutes."

"Sounds like a plan."

As we walked to the exit, I murmured to Fox, "Open my car door and smile at me adoringly. I'm pretty sure someone in here just made a call, which means somewhere outside, a paparazzo could be waiting with a camera."

He squeezed my hand, letting me know he understood.

And as he held the door open for me, leaning over me, I actually wished for a brief moment that it was all real. That I had someone in my corner who did love me enough to protect me. Not because it was his job, but because he couldn't bear for us to be apart.

Fox laid a gentle kiss on my cheek then helped me in the car. My eyes closed briefly, relishing the feel of being cared for. But I had to steel myself against the feelings. This wasn't real. We *weren't* a couple.

A camera flashed, emphasizing my point. This was all for show. We pulled apart and I got into the car, exhaling a long breath as Fox closed the door to the outside world.

Show's over, folks.

One event down and many more to go. I asked for Fox's cell and logged into my Instagram account. After getting a pose of my hand and taking the picture, I uploaded the photo and added a caption.

Happiest day of my life!

#heputaringonit #happilyeverafter #tiffanys #happiness #love #herecomesthebride

THE PROPOSAL VIDEO AND THE PHOTO OF MY ENGAGEMENT RING went viral in a matter of minutes. My publicist had already been warned and had a statement prepared for when news sources started calling. Now my upcoming nuptials to Fox played on every channel touting itself as *news*, especially the entertainment and celebrity so-called news sources. The coverage mystified me. Couldn't they report something actually newsworthy?

And Fox had been right.

The public loved the bodyguard aspect of our "romance." As if we were a real-life fairy tale come true. I'm not going to lie. I may have thrown my phone across the room at the constant *The Bodyguard* GIFs rolling through the Twitterverse. You'd think a movie from 1992 would be safe from being immortalized as a GIF. Nope. All I had to do was get engaged to Fox for the trolls to hijack my feed.

I hadn't been able to see Holiday and Tavia yet, and I missed them fiercely. Now that Fox's plan was in motion, doubts I thought I'd laid to rest were resurrecting. I needed my friends to convince me this whole scheme wasn't crazy but based on sound logic. Unfortunately, I had to postpone spending time with them yet again. Fox was taking me out tonight so we could display our "happy couple" status and let people take pictures of us.

Whatever that was supposed to look like.

A knock sounded on the bedroom door, and I sat up, smoothing a hand down my dress. A quick pat assured me my blonde pixie wig was in place. Since I'd just dyed my hair brown, I didn't want to add more chemicals to it and risk damaging my tresses to return it to my signature color. Hence the wig.

"Come in."

The door swung open and Sasha stood there, hands gripped tightly.

"Is everything okay?" I rushed to her side, ushering her to the bench at the foot of the bed.

"I don't know," she whispered.

"Where's Fox?"

"In the living room talking to Grand."

"Is Miss Etta okay?"

Sasha nodded.

I felt my brow furrow. What exactly was the problem? "Talk to me, Sasha."

"Are you really marrying my uncle?"

Oh. I shook my head and Sasha's shoulders drooped. "I didn't think so."

"I'm sorry. He thought it would help me…" My voice trailed off. I wasn't sure how much Fox wanted her to know.

"Help you how?"

"Never mind." I waved a hand. "That's not important. But I do need people to believe it's real."

Sasha bit her lip. "Then I can tell kids at school you're dating my uncle?"

Here it came. Someone always wanted to use me for something. My shoulders tensed as I waited for the real reason Sasha sought me out. "Well, the world believes we're engaged, so of course you can. But you know you can't say I'm staying here, right?" *Please don't put my life in jeopardy for fifteen minutes of fame.*

"I would never do that." Vehement objection flew from her lips as she squeezed my hand in a death grip. "It's just these girls at school think they're better than everyone because they can afford the latest kicks and newest iPhone. They make my life a living—"

Sasha bit her lip, abruptly cutting off a choice word. She sighed. "Anyway. I thought if I could maybe show them that selfie we took, they'd stop picking on me."

My heart turned over. "Oh, Sasha. Why didn't you tell Fox?" He'd be at the high school the first chance he got if he knew his niece was being bullied. He lived to protect.

"He has an important job already. I didn't want to bother him." She shrugged as if it was no big deal.

But I remembered how catty girls in high school could be. I sighed. "I have an idea." I examined her fresh face. "Have you ever worn makeup?"

She shook her head.

"Let me make you over. Then we'll post a selfie online, 'kay?"

"Really?" The look of yearning on her face pierced me straight through.

When was the last time she'd had honest-to-goodness girl time? "Really. Plus, your uncle and I are going out tonight, and I need to look pretty." I gave her a wink.

"You always do."

My heart warmed at her sincerity. "As do you. Don't let anyone tell you differently, all right?"

Sasha nodded.

I got to work, pulling out my makeup from my duffel. What could I say? I may have been prepared to run, but not without the essentials. Soon, I had a purifying mask on her face as well as mine while we talked about the latest fashion trends. Which ones we liked and which ones we hoped faded soon. We scrolled through Pinterest and magazines on our cells while the masks did their work.

I couldn't remember when I'd had so much fun. After removing the purifying mask and going through the whole process again with a moisturizing one, I artfully applied makeup to both of our faces. Soon we were posing and laughing at the different filters available on her camera app. Sasha scrolled through the pics on her phone, and we looked at each one before deciding on the perfect one.

I pointed. "This one. You look beautiful, not overly done, and your eyes are so radiant in this picture."

Fox's eyes. *Always Fox.*

"Thank you," Sasha gushed. She selected it and looked at me. "What should I say?"

"Here, can I?" I asked, holding my hand out for her phone.

She smiled and passed the cell to me. My thumbs flew across the screen as I wrote the caption, tagging my Instagram account and the makeup brands we'd used. I showed her what I'd written.

Hanging with my future aunt. We had some much-needed girl time before she hits the city tonight to celebrate with my uncle.

#makeup #NaturalBeauty #beauty #girltime #picoftheday #blackgirlmagic #blackisbeautiful #blackexcellence #black-girlsrock #beautifulwomen #blackbeauty #melaninpoppin #melaninmagic #melaninqueen

"I love it, Tori." Sasha beamed.

"Great. Go ahead and post it."

Her phone began pinging with notifications of all the likes and comments she was receiving.

Sasha's mouth dropped. "The likes are coming in so fast!"

"Stalkers," I quipped, wincing inwardly at the truth of the statement. Not that everyone was a stalker, but knowing I had one brought an eeriness to my comment.

Chills slipped down my spine and I swallowed, mouth suddenly dry. "Well, I need to get dressed for tonight."

"Of course." Sasha stood. "Thank you again. I had so much fun."

"So did I. It's been a while since I could relax and just have fun. Thank you." I reached out for a hug on impulse.

Sasha went stiff and then her arms wrapped around me tight, squeezing me hard. I couldn't help but wonder if she missed her mom. Did Miss Etta talk about the things her mother would have talked about? Did Sasha miss having a shopping partner?

I pulled away and peered down at her young face. "If you ever need to talk, you know where to find me, 'kay?"

She nodded, her eyes glassing over. "I'll let you get ready," she croaked.

"Bye, sweetie."

Her fingers wiggled at me as she walked out. I needed to introduce the girls to Sasha. In our gab fest, she'd told me how big a fan she was of both Holiday and Octavia. If I could find some way to treat her to some more girl time with my besties along for the fun, we'd have an epic time.

I threw on a fitted, long-sleeve black dress that stopped mid-shin. Fox had made a way for me to stop by the townhouse to grab more clothing, since my professional engagements were back on the calendar. He'd made sure that Tavia and Holiday wouldn't be there, so we didn't have to worry about putting them in harm's way.

I opened my travel jewelry box and grabbed a pair of dangling diamond earrings that would go perfectly with my jewel-encrusted Jimmy Choos. The slingbacks always made my legs look leaner and longer. A must for a model. I added a three-diamond necklace to complete my look.

Moving forward, I turned my head left, then right, checking out my wig. Should I stay with the blonde pixie or switch to one of my other wigs? Or even go out with my natural brown cut showing for the world to see? One thing about this night had to be authentic, I pulled off the wig and made sure my natural hair didn't need any repairs. All of me had to appear supermodel-worthy.

When I was done, I nodded in satisfaction. "Fake engagement, take two."

❧ 11 ❧

THE CITY SKYLINE SPARKLED IN THE NIGHT SKY, BUT THE bedazzling lights had nothing on the restaurant's atmosphere. Chandeliers dripped from the ceiling in opulent elegance, giving romantic lighting to each table in the Michelin star bistro. The smells wafting from the kitchen set my mouth watering, overriding the nerves that had been building at the knowledge we'd be on full display as a couple. Then again, there was a Grammy-winning singer making googly eyes at a man who wasn't her boyfriend. Maybe they'd take center stage on the tabloids and move Fox and me off.

Fox reached across the table, palm up, and I slid my hand into his. I couldn't prevent the quiver in the pit of my stomach, and I hated that the attraction pulling me toward the man in front of me wasn't pretend. My forced smile wobbled before I relaxed into one of contentment.

A camera flashed off to my left, and I barely suppressed a roll of the eyes. When I was at a photo shoot, I expected to have hundreds of pictures taken of me, but was it too much to hope for a modicum of privacy out in public?

"Keep smiling and remember why we're doing this," Fox murmured.

I nodded, letting out a breath. "You're right. I don't know why I'm so tense tonight."

"Playing a part can be exhausting."

I peered into Fox's eyes. "When have you ever played a part?"

"Everyone has to at least once."

"Why do you do that?"

"What?" His thumb began to make lazy circles on the back of my hand.

Little pinpricks of heat shot through me with each caress. The urge to yank my hand back and place it in the safety of my lap rose with each stroke. Did he know the effect his touch had on me? Was he as affected by me as I was by him?

I drew in a deep breath. "Why do you give me cryptic answers when I ask you a question? I'm not going to tell anyone your secrets, so you can be a little more open with me."

"Like you are?"

Touché. Still, I wanted to know. "Seriously, Fox, why do you hold everyone at arm's length?"

"Not everyone." He sighed, then looked directly at me. "Look, I have a job to do. My duty is to keep people safe. If I let anything or any*one* distract me, then I'm ineffective and people could get hurt. I *have* to stay focused."

My face heated with shame. "I'm sorry. I just wanted to get to know you a little better, have a nice conversation." Curse my need for connection.

Fox bowed his head as if in prayer, but we hadn't received our order yet and the sliced baguette wasn't worth a prayer in my opinion.

When Fox looked back up, his gaze held me captive. "Tori."

My eyes widened. He'd used my first name instead of calling me Princess. What did that mean? "Yes?"

"I *have* to keep you safe. If I ignore a question or deflect, then I'm doing so for your safety, to remain aware. Promise me you'll always remember that. *Everything* I do is to keep you safe."

I nodded, but my mind whirled. There seemed to be some kind of hidden meaning behind his plea, but I couldn't figure him out. Then again, maybe there was no subtext, only wishful thinking on my part. Because, even though I didn't want a relationship, I wanted Fox to like me. It was pathetic and I would so groan and make all sorts of rude comments if this were a movie or TV show.

But living it in real life was something entirely different.

We carried on the show of harmony and contentment, sticking to surface conversations that would allow Fox to maintain a vigilant eye. After passing on dessert and paying the check, we rose, and headed out of the restaurant. Once outside, Fox rested his hand on my hip, tucking me into his side as we waited for the valet to bring the SUV around. I wrapped my arm around his back and leaned into him.

Anyone watching would think we were enjoying a nice cuddle, but they'd be wrong. I could feel the tension in Fox's body as he stayed on alert. A chip fell off the wall surrounding my heart. How could I keep Fox from worming his way past my defenses? Not when the desire to be protected and cherished was my number one need.

Past experiences had taught me men were out to take, to fill a base need. That I was only worth my looks and nothing more. Yet, that knowledge didn't keep my heart from softening as I stood by Fox's side, being held and sheltered. Maybe there were men out there who didn't always take what wasn't theirs.

Tires squealed from somewhere down the road. My head popped up, turning toward the sound.

Fox shoved me behind his back and barked out orders. "Walk backwards until we're inside."

His broad shoulders blocked my view. The desire to peek

and know where the danger was coming from pricked me, but the urgency in his voice demanded I follow his orders without hesitation. Before I could take more than a few steps, Fox turned, wrapped me in his arms, and barreled toward the entrance of the restaurant.

Gun shots rang out. People screamed.

The door whooshed open, and Fox jerked as we crossed the threshold. He quickly moved us away from the glass pane. Others already had their cell phones out, hopefully trying to get emergency on dispatch and not create a live feed to be used by a media outlet.

People in New York were a lot quicker to pay attention to criminal activity since 9/11. Fox stood, his breath labored. I peeked up at him and frowned. Beads of sweat dotted his forehead. His mouth tugged down with a frown as his brow furrowed. Was he hurt?

"Were you hit?"

"Pretty sure I got winged."

Panic flared within me. "Winged?" I whispered harshly. "What does that even mean?"

"Just a nick. Calm down."

"A nick? You were shot?"

He nodded and my knees nearly buckled. "Did you call for backup?"

"I pressed the alert button to make the others aware. A couple of the guys were told to stay nearby and should be here shortly."

The door swung open and Jax, one of Fox's employees, rushed to our side. "All clear outside."

"He's been shot, Jax," I whispered.

Jax turned an assessing gaze Fox's direction.

"I was nicked. The bullet's not lodged in me."

"Then why are you sweating so badly?" Tension filled my body. Fox couldn't be hurt again.

"It took a piece of my side. Let it happen to you and see if you grin and walk around drinking lemonade."

"Grouchy, isn't he?" Jax smirked.

"Guess getting 'winged' will do that to you," I said, using air quotes. Winged my foot! He had to be seriously injured for him to sweat so much. "We're taking him to the emergency room, right?"

"Of course."

Fox grunted. "Please don't."

Jax pinned Fox with a glare. "You're too heavy to carry, so start acting like a man and walk under your own steam so we can get you some help."

Fox nodded, gritting his teeth and wincing as he straightened. I wrapped my arm around him so he could lean on me and I almost gasped when I felt a sticky substance against my fingers and a hole where part of his jacket used to be.

It certainly didn't feel like he'd been grazed, but what did I know about bullets? I didn't watch crime shows, and I refused to carry a gun. That's why my father had hired Fox in the first place. I swallowed and followed Jax to the idling car. Jax held open the back passenger door. I motioned for Fox to get in first.

"No. I'm your bodyguard, not the other way around."

"Men," I muttered, sliding across the leather seats. Fox soon followed while Jax went around to the driver's side. I buckled my seat belt and met Jax's gaze in the rearview mirror. Keeping silent, I held up my blood-covered fingers. He nodded and stepped on the gas, then handed me a handkerchief.

"Police will be at the hospital waiting for us."

"Thanks, Jax." Fox hissed as I pressed the handkerchief against his side. "That hurts, woman."

"Poor Mr. Bodyguard. I didn't know getting nicked could cause so much pain."

"You're a pain in my—"

I tutted. "Watch your mouth. I am a lady, after all."

Fox smirked, and I was glad he wasn't wincing in pain anymore. All I could think of was the time we'd been in the Town Car when a truck had come out of nowhere, ignoring his traffic signals and pretending like it was a night of Monster Jam. My hands shook as I remembered the sound of shattered glass.

I had walked away unscathed because Fox had used his body as a shield. He'd ended up with a broken wrist which, thankfully, was now fully functional. Tonight, he'd done the same thing again. A traitorous part of me wanted to believe I was special, but protecting people was his job. My father paid him handsomely to safeguard me.

"Are you okay?" I murmured, staring at his tie.

"I'll live."

"It's the small things."

He grunted out a laugh, and then a hiss of pain escaped.

"Sorry."

"Eh. Again, I'll live."

My heart pounded in my throat as I thought of the alternative. "I'm glad. I'd be dead twice over if it weren't for you." Tears clouded my vision.

"I'm good at my job."

And I was more than grateful. I cleared my throat. "How did you get so good?"

"Military."

My eyes flew to his. "You served?"

He nodded, not adding any extra information. I looked him over, trying to guess which branch he could have possibly been in. I knew a fellow vet would be able to tell with one look, but I sure couldn't. "Which service?"

"Navy."

See? I would have guessed Air Force or Army. "How long were you in?"

"Long enough."

"What does that mean?"

He let out a huff of air. "It means I'm in a bit of pain and really don't want to talk about it right now."

I looked away, nodding in understanding. His tone hurt though.

Never had a man made me so conflicted. Wanting to protect my heart against the onslaught of emotions he brought out in me, but wanting to be a part of his world so much I kept instigating conversation. Boy was I glutton for punishment.

Get over it, Tori. Remember the reasons why relationships don't work.

But my reasons were hard to believe in the face of my parents' upcoming thirty-fifth wedding anniversary. If two actors could last that long, then surely the rest of us mere mortals had a chance at having a thriving marriage.

Remember your scars.

The recollection was as effective as dousing cold water on my thawing heart. Enough to refreeze it and keep me from thinking *what if*. I placed Fox's hand on the handkerchief, then removed my own and scooted to the other side of the car. I may want him to open up to me, but vulnerability wasn't a favor I would be returning anytime soon.

THE DOCTOR AGREED THAT FOX HAD ONLY BEEN GRAZED. AFTER receiving a couple of stitches and a tetanus shot—I shuddered, remembering the size of that needle—Fox had been deemed good as new and sent home.

Phone-camera videos of Fox wrapping me in his arms at the restaurant's entrance and shielding me with his own body made the six o'clock news. The anchors speculated as to whether the shooting had been a targeted threat against me personally or a coincidence. I snorted. They needed to get in line. Fox, the police, and I all wanted to know the same thing. First Holiday—and inadvertently Emmett—now me.

The statistics had to be against so many horrifying coincidences. But instead of facing the thought, I'd buried my head in the proverbial sand—aka the tub. Sasha's bathroom wasn't as big as the one in my own home, but the water was extra hot, and the bubbles smelled fantastic. Miss Etta had given me a bath bomb a lady from church had gifted her. Apparently, she didn't do baths, which was another horror I couldn't contemplate.

I pulled the drain and quickly dried and dressed in jeans and a T-shirt. Although my body felt more relaxed, I couldn't still my brain. Fox had been shot because of me. Maybe staying and ferreting out my stalker hadn't been the wisest choice. I didn't want Fox or anyone else to die.

"Tori?" A soft rap of knuckles sounded.

Why couldn't Fox just leave me be? I didn't want to have to face him. Nevertheless, I moved in front of the door. "Yes?"

"You need to come out here."

I cracked the door open. "What's wrong?"

"Your dad's here."

My mouth dropped. "What?"

"He needs to know you're okay."

I closed my eyes. Where was I supposed to get the strength to face my father? Show him I was okay?

"Hey, you got this."

A shaky breath blew past my lips. "Right," I whispered.

"Come on."

I followed Fox down the hall.

"Tori!" my dad rasped.

He held out his arms, and I walked straight into them. Heat pressed against my closed eyes as I squeezed him as hard as he squeezed me.

"You're okay?"

"Mm-hmm." I nodded, burying my face into his topcoat. After a few more moments of soaking in his comfort, I shifted out of his hold. "How did you know where to find me?"

"Called Fox and let him know I *had* to see you for myself. No action report would suffice."

I shook my head. "You mean you demanded."

He shrugged, his salt-and-pepper eyebrows wrinkling with amusement. "Perhaps you know me too well."

"Where's Mom?"

"I made her stay home."

I arched an eyebrow. "How did you manage that?"

"Easy. I can blend in. She can't."

Too true. People always recognized her wherever she

went. But if Dad put on a fedora and his topcoat, people just figured he was another New Yorker.

Dad squeezed my hands. "We want you to come have dinner with us tomorrow."

I turned to look at Fox, who leaned back in the recliner. His brow was smooth despite the exhaustion shadowing his eyes. My gaze drifted back to Dad's. "I'm not sure that's a good idea."

"Don't say no on my account," Fox said. "I'll be fine tomorrow."

I bit my lip. "You got shot, Fox."

"Nicked, Princess. Even the doctor said I was fine."

Why did he have to be right? I turned back to my Dad. "Can the girls come?"

I'd spoken to them while Fox had gotten stitched up. If they didn't get to see me soon, they'd be the next guests in Miss Etta's apartment.

"Sure."

"Then we'll be there."

"Fabulous." He kissed my forehead. "Please be careful."

I nodded.

"Thanks again, Fox." My father shook Fox's hand. "Be sure to send me the hospital bill."

"I have insurance."

"I insist."

Fox grimaced but nodded.

"I'll see you two tomorrow."

And like that, he was gone.

"Why don't you have a seat?" Fox asked, motioning toward the couch.

"I think I'll go to bed."

"I need to talk to you."

The look on his face said it was important.

I shifted on my feet. "What's wrong?"

"Are you okay?"

"I'm tired." I couldn't help the curt tone of my voice. If I'd had my choice, I'd be far away from Fox to ensure his safety. Seeing him like this hurt, and knowing I was the cause had my emotions in a tailspin.

"Probably an adrenaline crash."

I snorted. "That left at the hospital. A cup of coffee righted me."

"Then why won't you look at me?"

"I'm. Tir-ed." If I could have stamped a dot on his forehead for him to get the implied period between those words I would've.

He folded his arms over his chest. "No, you're not."

I matched his stance. "Since when did you get an inside look into how I feel?"

"Since you started wearing your expressions on your face."

My arms slipped to my sides, a little snort escaping my lips. "Please. I have a fantastic poker face."

"No, you don't." He smirked.

"What do you want, Fox?"

"I already told you. I want to talk." He motioned to the couch once again.

"And yet I haven't heard anything significant come out your mouth."

He nodded as if my snippy replies had no effect. "You're angry."

My lips pursed. I could feel them bunching around the corners of my mouth, so I quickly neutralized my expression.

"Not fast enough, Princess. I know a ticked-off woman when I see one. I've been surrounded by them all my life."

"Hmm. Notice the common denominator? *You*."

He stood. "That's not fair. Don't project your emotions onto others and assume I go around upsetting people."

"And yet, that's the feeling I have around you ninety percent of the time."

A slow grin crooked the corners of his mouth. "And it's that ten percent I'm curious about."

I snapped my mouth shut, ignoring the shivers of awareness racing up my arms. "Can we just talk tomorrow? We can hash…well, whatever this is, then." My hands motioned between us.

"You'd like that. Give you time to cool down and put your mask in place. But I'm not going to let you. Have a seat like a grownup and talk with me."

"I don't want to." And dang it if I didn't sound like a child now. I could cheerfully throttle him. Not that I would, but still.

A calm expression covered Fox's face as if he could stand there all day or night, waiting for me to respond. I wanted to bite my lip, let my brow furrow as I thought, but he claimed to know all my tells, so I just stared right back, unmoving.

Why was he doing this? He hadn't wanted to open up earlier. What was his reasoning now? My stomach twisted with each thought as I tried to decide.

"Trust me," he murmured.

I sighed and walked to the couch, sinking into the cushions. Fox had kept me safe. He'd earned my trust, even if I didn't want to accept it so quickly. Because, as much as I trusted him, I didn't trust him to leave my secrets alone.

My eyes widened in surprise as he sat down next to me. "What?"

"Shh. Listen." He placed a hand on mine, stilling my desire to put space between us. "I was a Navy SEAL—"

"Are you serious?"

"Tori, for once in your life, don't interrupt."

I clamped my lips shut, nodding for him to continue.

He removed his hand. "Being a SEAL, you don't go around telling people what you do for a living. I learned to keep secrets so well I garnered more attention than I needed."

What did he mean? I wanted to ask, but bit down on my tongue to keep silent.

"Now I own a company where keeping secrets is just as important. I have an extensive clientele. And even though I've been covering your case since this summer, I still have other clients. I've had to hire other men to ensure the other clients are well protected." He huffed. "Long story to say I'm not used to sharing what's on my mind."

"I understand."

He tilted his head. "But you're still mad."

I needed to be. I couldn't let myself forget what happened when a guy discovered your weakness. And Fox was quickly becoming mine. "Not *mad*, per se."

He arched an eyebrow. "I'd hate to see you seriously angry then."

"It's rare." I could easily control my temper when I had to. I couldn't recall how many photo shoots I'd done where anger had burned hot because the photographer thought he could *sample* the art. I'm sure the FBI had a thick case file with those men. I mean, after all, any one of them could be my stalker.

"Then why did you shut down?"

My face heated under his direct gaze. "I had to."

"Come again?"

"Look." I sighed. "You're not used to sharing, and I'm not used to sharing."

"Then why do you keep asking questions?"

I chuckled, but it lacked humor. "It's a sickness. I can't sit in quiet. Just keep ignoring me. I'll be better for it."

He leaned in, his dark eyes drinking me in. "But what if… what if I want to let you in? Share some of my secrets?"

My breath hitched. Oh, why did he have to make such a tantalizing offer? "Fox?"

"Yes?"

"Go back to being obstinate. This is just pretend." And I needed to remember that. "It's better that way."

His measured gaze assessed me, as if searching the truth for himself. "Is it?"

No! "Yes." It had to be. My sanity depended on it. My head bobbed up, once, while my pulse drummed a staccato beat.

Fox stood, taking me in with a measured gaze. "For now."

He walked away, and I couldn't help but feel he took a little piece of me with him.

❦ 13 ❧

Fox drove me to the hotel my parents were staying in so we could have dinner with them. He looked absolutely dapper in a *Juste Luc* suit. I'd given myself more than one reminder that our relationship was all pretend. Nothing but business to ensure my safety. But it didn't help when he wrapped a protective arm around me as the doorman greeted us.

I smiled in delight at the opulence of the hotel. They knew how to bring class and warmth to the city.

"Tori!" My father rose from a chair in the lobby and headed my way.

I moved away from Fox and tilted my cheek up for my father's greeting. "Hey, Dad."

He placed a kiss on my cheek. "Everything normal out there?"

Did he mean did anyone shoot at us again? No, thank goodness. "Just fine, Dad."

"Good." He held out a hand for Fox to shake. "How you feeling?"

Fox's shoulders straightened. "I'm perfectly capable of doing my job, sir."

"I know, I know. I asked out of concern, not questioning your skills."

Fox nodded.

I glanced around the lobby. "Where's everyone else?"

"Your mother is fixing her face. Her words not mine." He chuckled and ran a hand over his beard. "Emmett said he and the girls would be here shortly. I already have a table reserved. I was just waiting for everyone." He pointed toward the hotel sign with the restaurant's name showing.

"Sounds good."

"Tori!" Holiday squealed.

I whirled around just in time for my best friend to crush me with a hug. We swayed back and forth. Holiday let me go and Octavia wrapped her dancers arms around me. Her slender frame and petite stature made me feel like I was hugging a child. The disparity between our heights usually cracked me up, but right now, I was simply happy to have my best friends surrounding me.

"I've missed you guys so much," I said on a choked whisper.

"Missed you too," Tavia said.

"Like crazy," Holiday added.

I sniffed and then looked at Emmett, standing behind Holiday. "How are you feeling?"

"All better." He opened his arms and I slid into them.

I was so happy to see my brother healthy and whole and recovered from the gunshot wound. He was my favorite person besides the girls. I'd been lucky growing up, never having to worry about my brother picking on me, pestering me, or making fun of me. Emmett had always been my best friend and my protector. Which was why he could never know what had happened—the incident that seemed to have been the catalyst for all the others. He'd think it was all his fault and that he'd failed me, but that wasn't true. The blame lay solely with me.

"You okay?" Emmett whispered, giving me a little squeeze.

"I am now." With his heartbeat steady beneath my ear.

"Is Fox treating you right?"

My pulse skipped as I thought of Fox telling me we'd revisit the conversation I'd managed to sidestep. I nodded against Emmett's shirt.

"Good. Don't run off again."

I chuckled. "I'm not seeking a stalker repeat anytime soon."

"I bet."

"My babies." I pulled away from Emmett at the sound of my mother's voice.

She looked stunning in a red wrap-dress, her brown locks flowing in loose curls. As she neared us, I gazed into eyes that mirrored Emmett's and mine—the famous blue-green irises that had labeled us as exotic and earned us way too much time on the newsstands.

"Hi, Mom."

She kissed my cheek. "Hey, beautiful." She reached out and squeezed Emmett's arm. "I'm so glad to have you two here in one piece."

If she started dabbing at her eyes, I'd have to search for some hidden cameras. Then again, people in the Waldorf Astoria tended to keep to themselves.

"Do you think a picture of us in this hotel is worth a million dollars?" I wondered out loud.

"Oh easily," Tavia chimed in.

Holiday chuckled. "Considering you were named after the hotel? Yeah, I'm betting people are trying to figure out a way to take a pic right about now."

"Let's head to the restaurant then." Dad held his arm out for my mom, who laid her hand in the crook of his elbow.

Emmett followed suit with Holiday, and Jax matched his steps with Octavia, which left Fox waiting to escort me.

"Don't forget we're engaged," he murmured.

I threaded my fingers through his. "I didn't."

The maître d' led us to our table, then relayed the specials before departing.

"What are you getting, pip?" Emmett peeked over his open menu.

Fox covered a laugh with a cough, and I glared, daring him to mention the nickname Emmett used on rare occasions.

"Please tell me it stands for pipsqueak," he murmured in his gravelly voice.

I remained silent as I fought to ignore the tantalizing scent of his cologne. He was way too close to me, and the urge to scoot my seat nearer pulled at me. So, I scooted toward my father instead.

Tavia spoke up on Fox's right. "Tori used to be short. Funny considering she's five ten."

"And now who's the short one?" I winked at Octavia.

She lifted her chin, looking just as regal as when she stood on stage in a tutu.

"I think I want seafood," Holiday announced, rubbing her hands together.

"Oh, that sounds good, sweetie." Mom grinned at Holiday.

I imagined she had wedding plans and grandchildren already forming in her mind. She'd cried when Emmett told her he and Holiday were engaged.

Our server came, and we placed our drink orders and requested a couple of appetizers.

Dad looked around at us. "Should we say grace before the food arrives?"

Fox slid his palm along mine, and I pretended the heat that radiated from him left me unaffected. Tried to fight the pull that had me leaning toward him.

Be strong. This is all pretend. You're not really engaged. You're certainly not in love.

I gulped as my mother's hand squeezed mine and the pressure reminded me of the ring on my left hand. But it didn't deserve to be there. This was all a show. I had to treat it like reality TV. Sure, real people were featured, but the puppet master was always behind scenes, pulling the strings.

My mother dropped her hand and I glanced up, realizing Emmett had ended the prayer. My cheeks heated. I hadn't meant to zone out. Even though I didn't believe like my friends, I never wanted to be rude or insulting. Good thing only I knew I hadn't paid attention.

Once our appetizers arrived, we all fell into a natural rhythm, filling our small dishes with food as conversation flowed between us. When the dinner plates were delivered, silence temporarily filled the air.

Emmett peered around the restaurant, then pierced Fox with a brotherly glare. "So, Fox, are you sure this engagement is a good idea? You've already been shot." He kept his voice low so it wouldn't carry beyond our table.

"Son." Dad dabbed his mouth, placing his napkin on his lap. "Now's not the time."

"It's all right, Mr. Bell." Fox studied Emmet. "Injuries are always a possibility. You know that."

"Yeah, but I thought this scheme of yours would allow you to catch the man."

Fox set his fork down and lowered his voice, leaning forward. "The fact that this guy shot at us a day after our engagement hit the stands *proves* this plan is going to work. I can guarantee he was aiming for me and not your sister. He'll be a little more careful now that he realizes he'll have to get through me to get to her. He doesn't want Tori hurt, just wants everyone in her life eliminated."

Emmett's face blanched, as did Holiday's and Octavia's. I peeked at Mom, who looked flushed. I wished I could reach for her hand and assure her I was perfectly okay. Or as well as one could be when one had a deranged stalker that apparently didn't mind brandishing a handgun.

Her eyes locked onto mine. "Maybe this isn't a good idea, Astoria."

I winced at the use of my full name.

"Couldn't have softened that blow, huh, Fox?" Emmett tossed his napkin on the table.

"You started it." I glared at Emmett.

Fox sighed. "I do apologize. I didn't mean to come across so harshly. I just wanted to emphasize how sure I am of this plan. We'll get him."

Chagrin dragged his lips downward. Not that I noticed how full they were. It's not like I wanted to kiss him or anything. My stomach twisted and I inhaled sharply. I shot up. "I'm going to hit the ladies' room."

"I'll come too." Holiday rose and followed me.

Fox nodded at Jax to tag along. Ugh, this was getting *so* old. Jax held up a hand and called out into the ladies' room, awaiting a response. When none came, he went and was back within a minute. "All clear."

As soon as the bathroom door closed behind us, Holiday pulled me to a chaise and we sat. "What is *up* with you, girl? You're jumpier than rain pounding the pavement."

I frowned at the mental image.

Holiday placed a hand on my arm. "Talk to me, Tor."

I huffed. "I don't know if I can pretend to be engaged anymore."

"Why? Because you like Fox and don't want to?"

"What?" I hissed.

Holiday smirked. "Oh friend, you forget how long we've known each other. I know when you like a guy."

"Fine. I like him." Shivers trailed down my spine. "But I could never date him."

"Why not?" Holiday studied me like she was searching for the status of my soul.

Part of me wanted to blurt out, *dark, depressed, and hopeless.* But even I could admit that was a bit dramatic. "I don't date."

"Again, I ask, why not?"

"Hol, please. Let me live in that blissful place of ignorance."

"But girl, you're living in denial and suppression. That's not healthy."

"Then what do you propose I do?" And did I really want to hear her answer or just continue whining?

"Stop trying to figure out the end game. You like a guy, *genuinely* like him. Enjoy that and all that comes with it."

Was she crazy? How could anyone enter a relationship without knowing the end result? Talk about asinine. "I think falling in love with my brother has short-circuited some of your brain cells."

Holiday chuckled. "Or righted my view of life."

I could admit she'd grinned a lot more since dating Emmett, especially now that they were engaged. Ugh. People in love were disgusting. "Fox and I aren't like that."

"And something tells me you're the reason why." Holiday tapped her chin. "I bet if you gave Fox a chance, he'd surprise you."

"Or hurt me." *Like all the others.*

"Tor." Holiday sighed and wrapped an arm around my shoulder. "Let that pain go. It's not what you want to build a shield out of."

"Why not? What could be better?"

"God's love. Let Him take care of your heart and handle the rest."

My heart ached. "I just can't," I whispered.

"Why? Why won't you?"

Beneath the makeup and airbrushed shots, I was a broken woman. Ripped to pieces by someone else's hands. "Because He gives second chances."

Sorrow filled Holiday's eyes. "And you don't think you deserve one? Or you don't want someone else to have one?"

I stood up. "Don't worry about it. I'll be fine."

"Tori," Holiday whispered.

I shook my head and walked out. I didn't want to talk about it. Had never talked about what happened that first time or the other incidents that only compounded my pain. And I certainly wasn't about to start. If God wanted to forgive people for their sins, that was fine.

Didn't mean I had to.

❄ 14 ❄

NORMALLY I LOVED A PHOTO SHOOT. THE OPPORTUNITY TO DRESS up or wear something less suited to everyday life brought out my fun side. To be able to inspire those who saw the photos. Embody the idea the photographer created in his mind's eye, or simply bring a product to life. I was art, but I wasn't. More like a vessel for art.

But this photo shoot would be different. *Very* different. McCall wanted Fox and me to set up professional engagement photos. She informed me multiple magazines had been in touch with her, vying for that front-cover spread and exclusive interview. She gave me a list with all their names and told me to choose someone.

My stomach flipped in a yoga pose and had me searching for Zen. I sat next to Fox and showed him the list of publications. "Which magazine do you want to be on the cover of?"

His gazed scanned the page from top to bottom. "I've never even heard of some of these."

"How can my fiancé not know magazines?" I shook my head. "They're my bread and butter."

Fox chuckled, his dark eyes lightening with amusement.

"If it means that much to you, Princess, I'll memorize every magazine you've graced the cover of."

For the first time, his use of Princess didn't irritate the snot out of me. Instead, tingles of awareness shot through me as his gaze pierced me. I opened my mouth to rebuke him with a rebuttal, but Fox placed a finger on my lips.

Heat puddled in my middle.

"Let's just have a nice moment without the snark and defense mechanisms."

I nodded, too aware the motion made his finger caress my lips. I stilled and pulled my head backward. "Fine," I whispered.

Something that sounded suspiciously like "that you are" fell from his lips. But my ears were already filled with the heavy beat of my pulse, and I wouldn't make the mistake of asking him to repeat himself. I barely had a hold on my emotions as it was. Holiday's suggestion of enjoying Fox played like an endless litany in my mind.

Fox read the choices wordlessly then pointed. "This one."

I tore my eyes from his handsome face. "Good choice," I croaked. *Enchantment* had a huge following of women wishing for their happily ever after. They would love engagement photos and the interview that would talk of our big day. *Our big fake day. Don't you forget.*

"Will you be able to show the world you're in love with me?" His honeyed voice fell on me like a caress.

I pushed away my feelings and pulled his words to the forefront. "Of course. I'm practically an actress when I'm in front of a camera."

"Makes sense, considering who your parents are."

And they had totally played their part last night. We'd looked like one big happy family, despite the danger Emmett and I had recently faced.

"They certainly taught me well. Plus, I have a degree in drama."

TONI SHILOH

"Really?" Interest flashed in his eyes, fixated on me.

"No choice."

"If you'd had a choice, what would you have majored in?"

I'd never given it much thought. "Maybe photography?" I shrugged.

"Like Emmett?"

I shook my head. "His pictures are more human oriented. He travels around, showing the plight of the world. I like to showcase relationships in my photos." Like the one I took of our parents dancing in their kitchen. Maybe one year I'd give it to them for an anniversary gift.

"Wow. Could I see your photos sometime?"

My heart stuttered. I'd never shown anyone my pictures. Not even Emmett. He knew I took them—everyone close to me knew I dabbled in photography—but no one had ever expressed an interest or the slightest suggestion my hobby could ever become something more.

"Maybe," I whispered.

"Thank you."

I nodded abruptly and stood. "We need to get our fake wedding plans underway."

"O-kay." Fox drew the word out. "Why?"

"The journalist for *Enchantment* will want to squeeze out every detail from us. We need to sound like we've discussed this, not like it's a whim."

"Valid point." He patted the couch cushion next to him. "So, let's plan."

"Right." I sat back down on the recliner. Where was my brain? Jumping up one moment, sitting the next. Fox completely muddled my senses. "Okay, what kind of wedding do you want?"

"Small and intimate," Fox replied.

Something in his voice made me pause. Was he being serious or just saying anything for the purpose of our ruse? "In a church?"

He tilted his head. "Not necessarily. God is everywhere, so I don't have to be in a church building for Him to witness it."

Goosebumps pebbled the skin on my arms. I'd never truly thought of God witnessing a wedding. And to think He could be anywhere, watching...oddly didn't give me a creep factor but a feeling of comfort. I swallowed. "Okay, small wedding anywhere." I made a note on my phone.

"Anywhere that will keep the intimacy of the wedding."

"Who would you invite?"

"Grand, Sasha, and the guys from work."

"Really? That's it?" I thought for sure Fox would have more friends.

"That's who matters. What about you? Would a small wedding be fine with you?"

I nodded. I could picture just the two of us, our immediate family, and our closest friends. I squeezed my eyes tight. *No, this isn't real. You're not* really *getting married.* Still, I couldn't shake the image of me in a wedding gown standing before him in a tux.

"Where would you want the ceremony and reception to take place?"

"620 Loft and Garden," I replied without hesitation. Their garden was spectacular, and their views of Midtown couldn't be beat. Oddly enough, St. Patrick's Cathedral overlooked the garden.

God is everywhere.

I shivered.

"That place is amazing."

My head snapped up. "You've been?"

He nodded. "It's peaceful. Looks like we'll have it there. When?"

"We can't really pick an arbitrary date. Some reporter is bound to double check our statements."

"Would the employees give that kind of information out?"

Good question. I bit the inside of my lip. "Maybe we call

them, see if they have an opening, and ask them to keep it secret? Bribe them if we have to?" But why did that have my stomach going up and down like a roller coaster on Coney Island?

"You know we can cancel a reservation."

"But they might charge a fee." Not that I cared, but I needed some kind of excuse to keep this from feeling real.

His mouth twisted in contemplation. "Call them anyway."

"All right." I unlocked my phone, typing their name into the search engine so I could pull up the contact details from their website.

"Rainbow Room, this is Trish. How can I be of service?"

"Hi, I'm interested in reserving the Loft and Garden for an event."

"Wonderful. Let me transfer you to our events coordinator." Hold music filled the line, soothing notes from a guitar.

I bet Holiday could play better music. Finally, the coordinator came on the line, introducing herself. I repeated my request.

"What type of event?"

"A wedding."

"Oh, congratulations."

I smiled even though she couldn't see my expression.

"Our next opening is November fourteenth."

"And how much to reserve?"

She named a figure that made me blink a few times. "That's not terrible. It would give me a little over a year to plan."

"Oh, no." She said in a rush. "That's this November 14th. We had a cancellation."

My heart stuttered. "A cancellation?"

"Yes. Unfortunately, it does happen. And if you were to cancel, you'd get back twenty percent of your down payment. We don't always recoup our loses."

"Oh."

I looked at Fox, who arched an eyebrow at me. I muted the phone. "They have an opening for November. You know, the one in a couple of months, *not* next year."

"Book it."

"Really?" My heart did a strange flip.

"Your stalker will lose it when he reads that we're not planning on a long engagement. Trust me. This will flush him out."

I exhaled. This all felt...too real.

"No arguing, Princess. Book it."

"Fine," I snapped. I unmuted the event coordinator and told her I'd take the spot.

"Great. Can I get your name?"

"Can I trust your discretion?"

"Of course. We pride ourselves on our privacy policy."

I gave her our names and sighed in relief when she didn't make a fuss. Maybe they really could be trusted.

"Perfect, Ms. Bell. And your credit card number?"

I rattled off the digits, ignoring the somersaults going on in my stomach. *This. Is. Too. Real.*

"Fabulous. I'll send you all the information you'll need, including a list of our approved vendors and a contract for you and Mr. Fox to sign."

"Thank you."

"My pleasure."

I hung up and stared at my cell. We had a venue, an engagement ring, and an upcoming photo shoot. How was this pretend again?

MELODY, THE *ENCHANTMENT* JOURNALIST QUICKLY REACHED OUT to us in order to schedule the photo shoot and interview. Now Fox and I stood on *Top of the Rock*, Rockefeller's observation deck. This spot had been an engagement photo backdrop more times than anyone could possibly count, but I didn't mind. This was New York, and the public probably expected pictures that exemplified that. Plus, all the people who'd buy the magazine would eat it up.

Fox wanted a casual theme to our photo shoot, so we both wore white T-shirts, though his contoured to his body like a glove and mine cut in at the waist then flowed at the bottom. Our matching outfits continued with dark-wash jeans and sneakers on our feet. The only bit of jewelry I wore was my aquamarine engagement ring. The beauty gleamed in the sun's light.

At the photographer's request, I gazed into Fox's eyes as he stared down into mine. Our gazes locked and all other noise faded away. For once, I couldn't read a photographer's mind, let alone hear anything he had to say. Had no idea what he wanted other than for me to look into Fox's eyes.

"Relax," Fox murmured, giving my waist a squeeze.

How could I when every cell in my body was aware of how close we were to each other? Of how we fit? How Fox felt like safety, home, and that *l* word that couldn't describe us.

"I can't," I whispered back.

Fox slid his hand up my arm and cupped my face. "Just you and me. Nothing else. Trust. Me."

My breath caught in my throat, and I sank into his arms. Surrendering for a moment. Only a moment.

"Yes! Perfect."

My eyes widened at the photographer's shout of happiness, but Fox gave a slight shake of the head. "You and me, Princess. Focus only on you and me."

I wasn't sure how long we stood there, but after a few pose changes, we were finally done. Fox wrapped his hand around mine as *Enchantment's* journalist came forward.

"Those pictures are going to look amazing." She beamed. "You ready for the interview?"

No! I nodded and Fox answered, "We're ready."

"Great. Let's go this way." We followed her to the elevator, and she pushed a button next to one of the listed restaurants.

After we'd settled into a corner table and ordered drinks, Melody pulled out her tape recorder. "Do you mind if I record this?"

I gave her my public persona smile. "Go ahead."

"Our readers are going to want to know how you two even fell in love. The model and the bodyguard...it's so 1990s and absolutely adorable. When did you know he was the one?"

I peered at Fox, and his lips quirked. He seemed to be saying *you and me.* Taking a deep breath, I looked back at Melody. "I couldn't stand Fox when I first met him."

A gleam entered Melody's predatory journalistic eyes. "Do tell."

I leaned forward as if sharing a conversation with my

bestie and not a well-paid just-above-tabloid writer. "You see, my father surprised me by hiring Fox. I didn't believe I needed protection. But when I yelled at him for calling me Princess—"

"You didn't!" She gasped.

"Oh, she did," Fox interjected.

I winked at him, loving how his grin grew bigger in response. I turned back to Melody. "He fussed right back, and I was surprised."

"Why?"

"No one talks to me that way." I sat back in my chair. "I've been put on a pedestal by so many people, and Fox treated me like a regular person."

"And that was it?"

"That was it. To so many people, I'm this superstar who they think has it all together. Most people I interact with don't treat me like a regular person, but Fox gave me that back."

"I just love how you call him Fox and not Marcel. Do you only call him that in public or in private as well? Do y'all have any pet names for each other?"

Melody was spitting out questions faster as her excitement built.

"Tori will always be Princess to me." Fox squeezed my hand under the table.

"But doesn't that bother you?" Melody's blue eyes widened. "Doesn't that seem a little antiquated."

"Oh, at first it got under my skin. So bad." I made a mock angry face, shooting it Fox's way. "Now it's become an endearment. I could tell he had feelings he didn't want to admit to when the way he said it changed." Not a total lie. He had said it softly the other day.

Then again, it could have been all for show, just like this. Part of me wanted the look in his eyes to be real. To admit that I was falling for my bodyguard and felt safe in his arms. To believe that he saw beneath the fake smile I brushed across my lips for onlookers to the heart that beat within my chest.

To be known, really known, was all I'd ever wanted.

"Oh, that's so romantic." She motioned between the two of us. "Have you seen the Twitterverse ship your names? They've got some suggestions going."

Sasha had shown me a few yesterday, so I nodded.

"Uh, what do you mean ship our names?"

Melody threw her head back and laughed. "Oh goodness. Guess you don't pay attention to couple names. Like Brangelina?"

"Gotcha. What are some of the suggestions?"

"Tarcel, Marceri, Marcori, and those are all combining your first names. For last name suggestions they've got Fell, Foell, and Beox."

Fox shook his head. "Some of those are terrible."

"Then what would you suggest?" Melody tilted her head, studying Fox.

"Hmm."

"Fri?" I threw at.

"Nah."

"Foori?"

Fox's lips turned down at my suggestions. "How about Bex? Uses our last names."

"Bex is adorable," Melody proclaimed with a clap of her hands.

"Bex it is." I grinned. It actually was kind of cute. "Our fans can call themselves Bexters."

"Done!" Melody chuckled and wrote a note down. "That's definitely going in the article." She looked up and motioned between us. "None of this feels kind of fast?"

"No." We said in unison.

"Have you set a wedding date?"

"Yes."

"Well?" she squealed. "When's the big day?"

I glanced at Fox. "Should I tell her?"

"Hmm, you might want to before she combusts."

I chuckled. "November 14th."

"Aww, I love fall weddings. And 2021 is the technical start of the new decade."

"Actually…" Fox murmured.

Melody's gaze darted from me to Fox and back to me. "What? What is it?"

"Oh, nothing." I smiled to put her at ease. "He's just trying to let you know you have the date wrong."

Melody frowned, looking down at her notepad. "I wrote November 14th."

"Yes, but it's this year, not next."

Her mouth dropped open. "*Shut. Up*. That's so soon."

"Our venue had a cancellation, and we couldn't let the opportunity pass." Fox gazed into my eyes. "It's going to be the perfect day."

Melody clasped her hands to her heart, looking like a real-life GIF of Kristen Bell. "You two are just adorable. Hashtag marriage goals."

I suppressed a bout of laughter.

After that, the rest of the interview flew by. I was surprised by the ease of my answers. They just sprang forth almost as if I really had fallen in love.

As Fox drove us back to his grand's place by way of mindless turns and back pedaling, silence filled the car.

"You did well," Fox said, turning to smile at me briefly.

"So did you."

"I almost believed you liked me."

"Maybe a little." I pinched my forefinger and thumb close together.

"That's a relief." He chuckled. "I was beginning to think I was the only one with feelings."

My head snapped around to stare at his profile. "What?"

"I think we make good friends."

Friends? Was he serious? My face heated in indignation. Friends was the last thing I thought about when I was close to him. My heart wanted so much more. *And your heart is stupid. You can't get involved. That's not the plan.*

I swallowed. Which meant friendship was the only viable option. That or keep him away from me with a proverbial ten-foot pole.

"Friends, huh?" I exhaled slowly, rolling the thought around.

Fox parked and turned to me, hand out. "Friends."

I slid my hand in his and shook. "Friends."

Yet my heart hammered loudly in my chest as warmth spread from our clasped hands to my heart. Being just friends might very well be my downfall.

❧ 16 ❧

MCCALL CALLED ME IN HYSTERICS. I NEVER WOULD HAVE thought my fearless agent could be ruffled, but apparently my stalker managed the feat. He'd delivered her own 8x10 headshot riddled with bullet holes and an ominous note demanding my whereabouts.

Fox ordered me to stay with his grand so he and his team could navigate the investigation with law enforcement. I hated sitting around doing nothing. Miss Etta must have realized my predicament, because she ordered me to help her bake some bread. Which is how I found myself punching dough as all my frustrations slowly seeped out.

"When you going to put that luggage down?"

My head whipped toward Miss Etta. "Excuse me? I unpacked my first day. I don't like wrinkly clothes." And still, my obsession with looking good for the public meant I often brought out the iron.

"Nothing a hot iron can't fix."

See?

"But that's not what I'm talking about." She pointed a flour-covered finger at me. "You've got no business carrying hurts the Lord wants to heal."

I schooled my features. I adored Miss Etta, but I didn't want to be preached to. Thankfully, Holiday and Octavia understood. Even Emmett hadn't pressed the issue of church until I'd lost that bet a few months ago. I'm sure he was upset my attendance didn't spark a conversion. Then again, Holiday did end up believing in God after the experience, so maybe some good came of it.

A Creator of the universe made complete sense to me. What didn't was His willingness to forgive all who sinned.

"Miss Etta," I started cautiously.

"Oh, don't you Miss Etta me. Your friends might be content to let this slide." She raised an eyebrow, her shrewd eyes studying me. "Or maybe they don't know how deep your hurt goes." She slowly nodded. "Yes, I see that now. And maybe that's why God brought you into my life."

"Why?" I couldn't deny the curiosity pulsing through me as knowledge filled her wise eyes. What did she see?

"Because He knows you need to hear some truth." She took the dough I'd been kneading and placed it in an oiled bowl, then covered it with a towel. She began washing her hands. "Let's go sit down and chat for a bit."

"But the bread…"

"Needs to rise." She gestured for me to wash up.

After drying my hands, I followed Miss Etta to the dining room and settled into a seat across from her. She clasped her fingers in front of her, leaning into her elbows as her gaze froze me in place. "It is not okay to ignore God, Tori Bell."

My mouth dropped. "I'm not—"

"Nuh-uh. No lies in this house. You'll be honest with me, and more importantly, honest with yourself."

I shuddered out a harsh breath. "How can I follow a God who forgives everyone, Miss Etta? Where's the justice in that?"

"Don't you know vengeance is the Lord's?"

I stifled the urge to roll my eyes. "Of course I do. Everyone's heard that. But I don't see any vengeance happening."

"It's not time. Child, everything has its time. You holding onto that anger, that unforgiveness…it's not right. God wants so much more for you."

I shook my head. "I have everything I could want. The best friends, a loving family. Enough money to satisfy my whims. I can get on a private jet and be anywhere in the world. Get the latest fashions."

"That's not what matters, Tori. You can't take any of that stuff with you when you're gone." Miss Etta stabbed her pointer toward her own chest. "This is what matters. And I'm afraid yours is as ugly as the sin you're holding onto."

"What?" I could feel my face scrunch up, the anger that simmered boiling a little higher. "*I* didn't sin. *I* was a victim." A lump formed in my throat. No, I didn't want to be anyone's victim. I leaned forward. "The ones…one who did this to me, he's the one who sinned. I haven't." I didn't lump the others with the first. The first one was the one who ruined my innocence.

"'But if you do not forgive men their trespasses, neither will your Father forgive your trespasses.'" Miss Etta paused, as if searching for the right words. "I'm not trying to preach at you or throw scripture like some holy weapon that would keep you from sinning. I don't know your hurt, dear girl, but I understand unforgiveness. Holding on to that bitterness cost me my daughter." Her eyes teared up, her bottom lip trembling with the force of suppressing her tears. When she started speaking once more, her voice was choked. "I'd give anything to go back and tell my daughter how sorry I truly am. That I shouldn't have kicked her out the house. Shouldn't have turned my back as she struggled to bring a child into this world."

I gasped. "I don't understand." Was she talking about Fox's mother? Or did she have other children? Had Fox's mother been forced to have an abortion when a door closed in her face? My stomach clenched, shock rendering me mute. How could someone as sweet as Miss Etta hurt another so deeply?

"When Mel told me she was pregnant"—Miss Etta dragged in a breath, a tear spilling onto her cheek—"I was very harsh with her. Lit into her on how I didn't raise her to be like that. Told her she wasn't a child of mine." She shook her head, sorrow drooping her head. "How I could hurt my baby like that, I'll never know. But I can't make excuses." She straightened up, looking me in the eyes. "Those were my words. That's how I felt. Chased her right onto the streets and told her to not come back." She wiped a gnarled hand across her face.

"How did you fix it?"

"I didn't."

Silence filled the room as my heart broke for Miss Etta's daughter.

"She died believing I hated her and wanted nothing to do with her. It was Fox's father that brought my grandbabies to me. Gave me custody of Marcel and Candace. They were my do-over. My chance to make it right."

Fox's mom was dead? Why hadn't he said anything?

"If I had been a little more gracious, a whole lot less stubborn, and if my heart had just been willing to forgive, I would have saved us both so much heartache. Not to mention been there when she died."

I wanted to ask about Mel's death, but my mind had too much to grasp. "I don't think our situations are the same."

"They're not. You're right. But unforgiveness is still unforgiveness. It hurts you, and depending on how long you let it fester, hurts others as well."

"No. I'm the only one who's been hurt. He got off scot-free." And it was a decision I regretted every day. But too much time had passed. Others would question the validity of my claim if I spoke out now. Not to mention the horrendous onslaught of publicity that would come with it.

"No. There *will be* a reckoning day. His crimes will not go unanswered."

"If I let this go, what will be left? I'll be defenseless." Remembering what happened made sure I didn't fall into the same traps. It was why romantic relationships were taboo. For one, I didn't want to reveal my deepest secrets and the pain that still clung to me. Second, how could any man truly be trusted?

"'But the Lord has been my defense, And my God the rock of my refuge.'" A soft smile covered Miss Etta's face. "'But You, O Lord, *are* a shield for me, My glory and the One who lifts up my head.'" Miss Etta reached across the table and took my hand in hers. "You see, Tori, you don't need any defenses. The Lord will be that for you and more. If you just let Him." She squeezed my hand. "Promise me you'll think about what I've said."

How could I not? My mind was reeling. The scriptures Miss Etta had said were ones I'd never heard. I didn't know how to think about anything else but what she'd told me. "I will, Miss Etta."

"Good." She rose, her knees creaking from the effort. "I'll go and rest before I finish the bread. I think I need some time with the Lord."

I watched as she left, my heart heavy for the heartache she'd endured. Surely I wasn't headed down the same path. I hadn't hurt someone close to me like Miss Etta had hurt her flesh and blood.

But aren't you hurting yourself?

It was something to ponder.

17

Knock, knock.

"Come in."

Fox opened the door, a grim look on his face.

"What's the verdict?" I sat on my temporary bed, my legs crisscrossed.

"We couldn't find any prints."

"And McCall?"

"Shaken but determined to keep you safe, despite the threats of harm if she doesn't deliver you to him."

I gulped. "So, he's escalating? That's good, right? Means you'll catch him soon, right?" Preferably before he made good on his threats.

Fox gave a nod. "I think we need to go out again. Create another media wave."

I winced, remembering the fiasco at the restaurant. "Will you be wearing a bullet proof vest this time?"

"Yes. We have thin models that are practically unde-tectable. But I did talk to Luc to make sure it will still fit under my suit and remain that way. He wants me to come in for a fitting."

"Good." I couldn't stand to see Fox hurt. Tore my insides

up more than I wanted to admit. But he'd slowly become my friend. It was normal to feel that way about people I cared about, right? *Just friends, Tor. Nothing more.*

Fox sat in one of the chairs and studied me. "You okay?"

I shrugged.

"Want to talk about it?"

"Maybe?"

He chuckled. "I can keep secrets, Tori. Lay one on me."

"What happened to your mom?" My eyes widened, and I slapped a hand over my mouth. I hadn't meant to ask that. Even if the question had been going through my mind since my talk with Miss Etta.

A muscle ticked in Fox's jaw. My body stiffened as I waited for the coming onslaught. I had no business asking him something so personal. Sure, we'd agreed to be friends, but we weren't on that level yet, and I deserved any disdain he'd throw my way.

"She died when I was ten."

My heart sank to my toes at the grief in his voice. "How?" I asked softly.

His Adam's apple bobbed, and he peered up at the ceiling. I sincerely hoped it was to think and not to hold back any tears. If he cried, I'd lose all composure.

"Drug overdose." His voice sounded raw. Ragged.

"I'm so sorry." I scooted forward, then stopped. Did Fox need a comforting touch or space? "You don't have to tell me anything else. It's none of my business."

His chin lowered, and his red eyes captured mine. "I want you to know. To understand."

I nodded, too stunned to speak. And slightly shaky from the pounding of my heart. "Then I'll listen."

"Thank you." His mouth quirked into a half smile. "Thank you," he repeated, clearing his throat. He slid his palms down his jean-clad thighs. "I don't know where to begin."

"Wherever's easiest."

"My mom had always been addicted to drugs. All my memories of my childhood recall days she was too high to get food on the table or even see me off to school. My father wasn't around but stopped by every blue moon to make sure I was still alive." He looked at me. "His words, not mine."

My heart turned over.

He cleared his throat. "Before my tenth birthday, my mom kept asking me what I wanted for a present. She said double digits were special. I'd always shrug because I knew we didn't have a lot of money to spend on nonessentials. Some nights I went to bed hungry and didn't have anything to eat until lunch at school. Then one day, it hit me. For my present, I could ask her to get clean. To stop using. So that's what I told her the next time she asked."

My breath suspended. "What did she say?" I asked on an exhale.

"Her face wrinkled in a huge frown. I thought she was going to say no, but she just kept staring at me. Then she leaned down and placed a kiss on my cheek." Fox stopped, a tear spilling onto his cheek.

My eyes immediately watered in response. Should I go to him? Hold his hand? Fear rooted me in place. I wasn't used to so much raw honesty and emotion from this man.

"She said, 'I'll do that for you. I love you, Marcel.'"

I knew from the shakiness of his voice and the heartache stamped on his face that it didn't end so well. But I had to know. Had to ask. "Did she get clean?"

"For about two weeks. I was so excited when I woke up on my birthday. I didn't care that I was double digits. I just wanted another day with the woman who had started reading bedtime stories to me and Candace. Who had kissed us goodbye at the bus stop and was there for us when we came home. I couldn't remember her ever being clean before, but those days…" His breath shuddered.

"What happened when you woke?"

"She was gone," he choked out.

Tears fell fast, and before I could comprehend my actions, my feet propelled me off my bed and my arms wrapped around his broad shoulders. His body shook as he silently wept, tears running down the curve of my neck, soaking my shirt.

My heart broke for him. For his past. For the loss of his mother.

Our heads pressed together as I continued to hold him, saying nothing. And what could I say? I didn't want to offer any platitudes or pithy statements that would do nothing to change his past. He'd been given the gift of seeing his mother clean, all for it to end on his tenth birthday. Nothing I could say would help that.

But I could let him grieve in my arms. Let him know he wouldn't be left alone to his pain.

Maybe I'd been wrong in keeping my past close to me and secreted away. Maybe I should share. But it had been so long since I'd allowed myself to be vulnerable, I wasn't exactly sure how to go about it. Was this even the right time?

No.

Fox's body stopped shaking as he began drawing in steady breaths. I kept my arms tight around him, waiting to see if he'd shift out of the hug to let me know he was okay. But instead of backing away, his arms curled around me and squeezed.

"Thank you," he murmured, sending whispers across the curve of my neck.

"That's what friends are for, right?" I kept my voice low.

"Are we really going to be friends, Tori?"

"We shook on it."

His arms tightened. "What if I want more?"

Longing hit me like a New York summer heat wave, and my arms instinctively tensed.

"Tori?"

"Don't." I shook my head, hoping he'd stop before he spilled any more of his secrets. "It's not a good idea," I whispered.

An ache filled my chest, one that made me immediately want to take my words back.

"Why not?"

"I'm too…" Broken. "…messed up."

His hands spanned the width of my back. "We all are."

I shook my head, pulling back. "Fox, I'm…I'm not good for you. You lean on God, and I'd like nothing more than to pretend He doesn't exist. You're good, and I'm selfish."

He placed a finger on my lips. "You talk too much, and I keep quiet more than I should."

I wanted to argue, but I knew from past experience the electric currents I'd feel if I moved.

"I'm not ignoring your faults. I'm not trying to downplay your past. But hear me when I say, we all have things we need to overcome." His dark eyes roamed my face. "Do you believe in God?"

I swallowed. "Yes," I whispered. "But I can't surrender to someone who forgives everything. I'm not the girl for you, Fox."

He considered me. "Maybe not right now."

My mouth dropped in shock. What was he saying?

His finger slid across my cheek, and then his whole hand cupped my jaw. "I see you. The woman who is fearless in the face of public scrutiny but goes out of her way to ensure her friends are happy. To the point you'll sacrifice your life for theirs. And while that's an admirable trait, I don't want you sacrificing anything for me unless it brings us closer together."

"Fox," I whispered.

"I'm here. I'll be waiting until you're ready."

Yearning drummed through me. I couldn't give in though. Had to ignore the need to belong. To have a person who loved me despite my faults and wanted forever. I couldn't be what Fox deserved.

"I'm sorry." I rose out of his arms despite every tug and pull that tempted me to stay. Before I could change my mind, I walked away, keeping my back to him. I drew in a ragged breath. Another. And one more before I felt halfway decent.

We had to go back to the plan. Remember why Fox had even knocked on my door in the first place. We needed to be seen in public. Needed to draw the enemy out. I swallowed. "There's a fashion show tonight. I can get us tickets."

"Fine."

I winced at the hurt in his tone. I wanted to turn around and beg him not to hate me, but maybe it was better if he did. For him not to fall for me, so we could both leave this stalker situation with our hearts intact. Because if I yielded, there was no guarantee either of us would come out unscathed.

18

THE CONVERSATION WITH FOX REPLAYED OVER AND OVER IN MY mind until I thought I would go mad. I had to find a way to stop my brain from obsessing, since there were still a few hours until we hit the fashion show. My mind would explode if I didn't put a stop to its processing.

I opened the group text between Holiday, Tavia, and me used whenever we wanted to text everyone at once. If only I could curl my legs underneath me on the plushy sofa in our living room and have a face-to-face conversation with them. I felt adrift and in need of their wisdom.

T: FOX AND I HAD A MOMENT.

H: DO TELL!

O: A GOOD ONE OR A BAD ONE?

Excellent question, considering it felt like a wrecking ball had demolished my organs.

T: I DON'T EVEN KNOW.

H: DO I NEED TO SIC EMMETT
ON HIM?

O: ARE YOU OKAY?

I sighed, battling the pain that had been building.

T: DON'T TELL EMMETT. THAT'S WHY I TEXTED YOU TWO.

H: I was just teasing.

O: But are you okay?

T: I don't know. He wants more than I can give.

H: In what way?

T: He wants a relationship.

O: Aww. Sweetie, it's time to date again.

H: Way past time.

I shook my head. They didn't get it. *But how can they when you haven't told them?* I took a deep breath, thumbs flying across my cell screen.

T: You don't understand how messed up I am.

O: What do you mean?

H: I think we should FaceTime.

No! Earlier, I'd wanted nothing more than to see their faces, but if I had to let my darkest secret see the light of day, then being hidden via text was the only way I could do it. I didn't have the courage to look into their eyes.

T: Let's just continue texting.

H: Tor...

O: If you promise to talk to us.

I'm worried about you.

T: Okay, let me type this real fast.

H: We'll wait.

O: What Hol said.

I began typing.

T: Something happened in high school that I never told you about. I couldn't. Too ashamed.

Bouncing dots waved across the screen. I wasn't sure who was typing, but I needed them to wait before they asked questions.

T: Just give me a moment to type it all out.

The waving dots disappeared.

T: Do you remember the photography teacher?

T: Well when I took a class from him he always complimented me on my photos. Told me I had natural talent.

HE LET ME USE THE DARKROOM WHENEVER I WANTED. PUT ME ON THE YEARBOOK COMMITTEE AND ASSIGNED ME THE BEST CASES. I THOUGHT NOTHING OF IT.

And what a fool I'd been to believe his attention had anything to do with talent.

T: THEN ONE DAY HE GOT THIS LOOK IN HIS EYE AND TOLD ME HOW BEAUTIFUL I WAS. AND HE CARESSED MY FACE. IT WAS SO BRIEF I COULD HAVE IMAGINED IT. I THOUGHT I HAD WHEN HE STARTED TALKING ABOUT AN UPCOMING ASSIGNMENT.

H: HE WAS PLAYING MIND GAMES WITH YOU!

I'M GOING TO FIND HIM AND THROAT PUNCH HIM.

O: HUSH, HOL.

I chuckled through the pounding in my head and heart. Those two were so different, but love bound us together. I could only hope they wouldn't hate me for keeping silent all these years.

T: THE FOLLOWING WEEKS WERE MORE OF THE SAME. I'D WORK HARD IN CLASS. HE'D COMPLIMENT ME. BUT THE TOUCHING BECAME MORE OBVIOUS. AFTERWARD, HE'D ALWAYS BRING UP A SCHOOL ASSIGNMENT SO THAT I WAS LEFT WONDERING IF I'D IMAGINED THE WHOLE ENCOUNTER.

H: A THROAT PUNCH AND A KICK TO HIS MAN PARTS.

T: THREE WEEKS AFTER ALL THE WEIRDNESS STARTED, HE KISSED ME. I PUSHED HIM AWAY, BUT HE JUST CHUCKLED.

O: OH NO!

T: I STRUGGLED WITH HIM AS HE GRABBED AT ME. I FOUGHT BACK BUT HE WAS STRONGER.

My pulse quickened at the memory. An acrid taste filled my mouth and as my insides churned.

T: HE GOT MAD, BUT HE WAS CAREFUL. DIDN'T STRIKE ME IN THE FACE, ONLY WHERE NO ONE WOULD SEE. FINALLY I MANAGED TO KICK HIM WHERE IT MATTERED. I LEFT HIM ROLLING AROUND ON THE GROUND AND CAME STRAIGHT BACK TO THE DORMS.

My hands began to shake like they had that day. The shame that drowned my spirit wrung out my insides. And always, the questions flashed in my mind. Had I'd done something, said something, to make him think I'd wanted his attention? That I wanted *that?*

I hadn't said anything the first time he touched my cheek, after all. Kept silent the time after that. I'd never told him no or stop. But I had been so confused because he was my teacher. Never in my wildest dreams had I thought he was slowly grooming me to take advantage of me. Hadn't even heard of the term till a late-night internet search gave me insight into what I'd experienced.

I sniffed back tears.

O: WHY DIDN'T YOU TELL US, TOR? YOU HAVE
TO KNOW WE WOULD HAVE BEEN ON YOUR SIDE.

H: WHAT TAVIA SAID.

T: I THOUGHT IT WAS MY FAULT SOMEHOW.

I sniffed, trying to keep the tears from falling. Thank goodness I was alone and no one could see me unravel. I didn't even want my friends to see me relive the moment. Which was why I kept texting and ignoring their attempts to call.

H: THIS IS WHY YOU DON'T DATE?

T: IT'S A HUGE PART, BUT GUYS, HE ISN'T THE ONLY ONE WHO'S TRIED TO TAKE WHAT I DIDN'T OFFER. BEING IN THIS INDUSTRY, A LOT OF MEN THINK I'M WILLING JUST BECAUSE I MODEL. THEY CAN'T BE TRUSTED.

O: OH, SWEETIE.

H: I THINK DEEP DOWN YOU KNOW NOT ALL MEN ARE LIKE THAT. LOOK AT YOUR DAD AND EMMETT. FOX EVEN!

More dots danced across the screen, but I typed before the other text appeared.

T: I'M NOT SURE I COULD EVER OPEN UP TO FOX ABOUT HIGH SCHOOL OR ANY OF THE OTHER INCIDENTS.

O: YOU'RE SHARING WITH US. IT'LL GET EASIER THE MORE YOU TALK ABOUT IT.

I blanched. How many people did Octavia want me to tell?

H: Has Fox ever done anything to make
you believe he's not who he says he
is?

I stared at the text, stunned by the insight Holiday showed in asking her question so directly. Fox had never given me a reason to doubt my judgment where he was concerned. Well, sort of. I'd *thought* he was like all men, but he'd proven over and over that he was dependable and trustworthy. After all, I *did* trust him with my life.

T: No.

H: Then take that leap. Trust him with
your past.

O: I agree. Sometimes the thing we need
to do is not hold in our hurts. Share
them with others. Then they have less power
to continue hurting us.

Were they right? Could I really just let go years of pain and suddenly be free?

H: Have you considered praying about this?

T: No, but Miss Etta wants me to.

O: You should. I always feel so much better
talking things over with God.

T: I don't want Him to tell me to forgive that scumbag or the others who thought my looks granted them access to my body.

H: Oh, Tor. Forgiveness isn't for the Lord.
It's for you.

I heard her, but my anger didn't want to be released. It wanted vengeance and justice. If I forgave him, wasn't that just letting him get away with everything?

O: Did you report him?

T: No. I never did and I hate that I let him silence me.

AND NOW I'M IN THE PUBLIC'S EYE. I DON'T WANT TO BECOME ANOTHER HASHTAG.

H: BUT WHAT IF HE HURTS SOMEONE ELSE? WHAT IF NO ONE ELSE STOPPED HIM?

And hadn't that thought haunted me? A few years ago, I did a quick search at my high school alma mater to see if he was still employed. His photo was no longer in the staff directory, and my contacts had no idea where he'd disappeared to.

T: I'M NOT SURE I CAN SAY ANYTHING. HE DIDN'T RAPE ME. SURELY THE STATUTE OF LIMITATIONS HAS ENDED.

H: BUT THE GOVERNOR JUST SIGNED AN EXTENSION ON THAT. DON'T YOU REMEMBER? IT WAS ALL OVER THE NEWS.

T: THAT WAS JUST FOR RAPE.

Wasn't it?

O: HOLIDAY MIGHT HAVE A POINT. IT DOESN'T HURT TO TALK TO SOMEONE ABOUT IT.

Sure it did. Because then my face would be plastered all over newsstands with #metoo. I could ignore a lot of the media's speculation, but that...I didn't know how to react. Plus, I would have to tell my family so they wouldn't be blindsided by the money-hungry reporters.

T: GUYS, I CAN'T TELL YOU HOW MUCH I APPRECIATE YOU LISTENING AND CARING. I'LL THINK ABOUT EVERYTHING YOU'VE SAID.

O: I'LL BE PRAYING.

H: SO WILL I.

T: PLEASE DON'T TELL EMMETT, HOL.

H: NOT MY STORY TO TELL.

Relief flooded through me.

T: THANK YOU.

H: WE LOVE YOU.

O: SO MUCH.

T: LOVE YOU GUYS TOO. COME TO THE FASHION SHOW

TONIGHT. THINGS BETWEEN FOX AND ME ARE KIND OF AWKWARD. YOU CAN SIT BETWEEN US. 😊

H: LET ME CHECK WITH EMMETT.

O: I HAVE A CLASS TONIGHT.

I frowned. That meant Octavia was out. Not much could pull her from her ballet classes. She used them to keep her in prime condition and always said, "A ballerina never stops learning." I wondered how long she would continue to dance. Being that type of athlete put an expiration date on your career. She was already nearing thirty. Ancient in the world of ballet.

H: WE'RE OUT. EMMETT HAS A SURPRISE PLANNED.

T: ALRIGHT. I'LL TALK TO YOU GUYS LATER.

H: HAVE A GOOD TIME AND TALK TO FOX!

O: YOU'LL BE FINE. I HAVE FAITH.

At least someone did. Because telling my friends had been hard enough. How could I get up the courage to ever share with Fox? Staying in my current predicament seemed the best decision. Once the stalker was caught, I'd have no reason to see my too-handsome bodyguard again.

And maybe he'd fall in love with someone with less baggage. Someone who didn't walk around wearing distrust like armor. My friends loved me, but Fox didn't have to.

Just keep quiet.

❧ 19 ❧

WATCHING A FASHION SHOW WAS WORLDS DIFFERENT THAN BEING in one. Rather than the fast-paced changing in and out of designer couture, I could sit sedately and sip on a cocktail as the runway models did all the work. In fact, my only job tonight was to smile at Fox and discreetly flash my diamond engagement ring for photographers looking for an opportunity to exploit more than one model tonight.

Fox had his arm draped across the back of my chair and squeezed me close every time we exchanged words. I'm sure those watching thought we were hopelessly in love. I held in a snort, just as he turned to whisper in my ear.

"How long do we have to stay?"

"Until it's over," I returned his whisper.

He groaned. "Put me out of my misery, Princess."

A shiver of delight went through me. From his torture, *not* the faint wisps of breath that caressed my skin. "There's still another hour."

"Lord, help me."

"There's no getting out of this."

"What if I kiss you and then we get up suddenly?"

My insides turned to goo at the thought of his lips pressed

to mine. I cleared my throat. "Then it'll look like we're doing more than we are. That's not the reputation I'm known for."

"I can't believe..." His voice stuttered to a stop, and I turned to look at him fully.

Mortification had widened his eyes and deepened the area of his gorgeous cheek bones.

"I know you didn't mean to suggest anything more, but the eyes watching us will jump there."

He nodded. "Sorry."

I shrugged. The longer we played this game, the quicker he'd learn to think a few steps ahead of public perception.

We remained quiet the rest of the show, and finally Luc appeared on the runway, nodding his thanks to the round of applause. I stood alongside Fox and clapped, genuinely happy for the success of the show. Luc consistently put out the best designs and deserved all the recognition. He made eye contact with me and motioned me to come forward. I gave a discreet shake of the head. Even though I was wearing one of his designs, I wasn't in the showcase.

He made a bigger motion, using his head and hand to beckon me forward. The crowd had caught on and was now eyeing me in anticipation. I exhaled and strolled forward, pasting on a smile. Luc helped me up the runway and then used his hands—Vanna White style—to highlight the dress cascading down the length of me.

"Mr. Fox must join us," he said amidst the noise of the applause.

I caught Fox's gaze and hooked my pointer at him. He grinned and sauntered toward me. Dang if my heart didn't go into overdrive as those delicious grooves appeared in his cheeks once more.

He really could be a model with those cheekbones and dark eyes. The epitome of tall, dark, and handsome. I heard some gasps go through the audience as he threaded his fingers with mine and kissed my forehead. Ladies everywhere would be dropping like flies onto their swooning couches.

The crowd quieted and Luc stepped forward. "Merci, merci." He clutched his hands in front of himself. "Fashion has been my dream for so long. I want to thank the beautiful ladies and all who made tonight a success." He looked at me. "And I know some are wondering why I called these two up here. They are wearing the latest from my secret line, soon to be available to the public. You like the sneak peek, non?"

The crowd cheered.

"When will you get married?" someone shouted from the back. Most likely some reporter trying to get a promotion.

I flashed a look of apology to Luc for stealing his moment. He lifted his shoulders and tilted his head as if to say *what can you do?*

I turned toward the center of the crowd where I thought the questioner might be seated. "Read the next edition of *Enchantment* for more info."

"Kiss her!" a woman shouted.

My chuckle soon turned to dread when the mantra was repeated until the crowd chanted in unison.

Oh no. This couldn't happen. I turned to Fox, hoping the dread wasn't visible on my face and that I'd kept my public mask in place. Inside, my organs were knocking against each other as they all tried to flee from the thoughts imploding my brain.

Fox placed his hands on my waist. "We don't have to do this."

"They won't stop unless we do," I choked out. My heart was hammering so loudly, so swiftly, I'm pretty sure an EKG would show signs of a heart attack.

"I'll take care," he whispered.

I smiled to hide my nerves and leaned forward the same moment he did. We met in awkwardness, but then the warmth of his lips fissured through me. I stepped closer as he angled his head and continued to brush his lips over mine. His hands squeezed my waist as mine slid around his neck. Everything disappeared except the feel of his lips and the pleasure humming through me.

Heat ripped through me as I clung to his neck and kept the pace he'd set. He must have sensed my feelings, because he gentled the kiss, his hands now cupping my face. Slowly he drew away until our eyes met. Mine seeking. His intense. As if he was trying to tell me something.

"Proof there's more between us than you want to admit," he murmured softly, not an ounce of smugness in his tone.

I swallowed, trying to find my equilibrium.

"Welcome back, you two." Luc's voice sounded behind me and I jumped, whirling around to meet his mocking gaze.

Something that seemed awfully close to jealously lurked in his eyes. His gaze drifted to my right, as if to redirect me to the audience, who'd had a front seat showing at my first kiss with Fox.

"Right. Forgot they were there," I mumbled.

Luc's lips had flattened into a thin line. "We noticed."

Warmth flooded my face, and I waved to the crowd before taking Fox's hand to leave the stage. Fox guided us to toward our seats. Holes seemed to bore into the back of my head as I imagined the whispers and stares we were receiving. I had a feeling I knew what the topic of conversation would be once we got back in the car.

But I was wrong. Fox didn't say a word until he armed the alarm in Miss Etta's apartment. Instead of escaping to the guest room, I stood in the hall, waiting.

He turned and leaned against the door, his arms folded and his gaze assessing. I attempted to swallow, but moisture had left my mouth halfway through our ride home.

"Ready to talk about the elephant in the room?"

"That kiss changes nothing, Fox."

"Marcel." His voice was like steel.

123

I couldn't call him by his first name. It was too personal. Too…real. "I can't be who you need."

"You already *are*." His voice was low. Urgent. And the desperation underneath undid me.

My eyes watered, and I begin blinking rapidly. *Don't cry. Don't cry. Don't. Cry!*

Fox took a step closer, cradling the side of my face. "Whatever keeps you locked up tighter than the crown jewels, please, trust me with it. Let it go. Please, Tori."

My lip trembled, and a sob ripped through the silence of the night. He pulled me forward, wrapping his strong arms around me as my shoulders shook and tears erupted. I couldn't even fathom why they'd release, now, in this moment, but they did. And I was helpless to stop them. I ducked my head, placing my forehead against his chest, and cried. For every hurt I'd bottled up and pushed into the farthest corner of my mind.

Cried for the shame that had held me captive much longer than it ever should have.

Cried for not being baggage-free and able to say yes to him. To a relationship and a future.

I wasn't sure how long I stood in the comfort of his arms, but eventually I became aware that my tears had stopped and my arms were now wrapped around him. There was such a rightness in his comfort.

I straightened to my full height and nuzzled my face in the crook of his neck.

His hand ran soothing circles on my back. "All better?"

"I don't know about all better."

"Do you want to tell me what's going on?"

I didn't, but after sobbing my guts out, I supposed I should. "Okay," I whispered.

Fox pulled away, taking my hand, and tugging me toward the living room. He guided me to the recliner, so I sat, giving him a bemused expression. As if I didn't know how to get in a chair by myself. Then again, maybe he knew it was my favorite spot in the living room.

He squeezed my hand, then sat on the couch as if he knew by instinct that I would need the space. "I'm listening."

I nodded. Anxiety attacked my nose, an itchy feeling invading it. My eyes watered and my voice wavered. "I had an experience in high school that's left me a little leery."

More like a whole lot. I stared at my hands, even though I could feel Fox studying me. I didn't want to face him. If I could just get this all out, then everything would be out in the open, and I could safely retreat behind my wall.

"When I was in high school, I took all the photography classes they offered. It wasn't something I thought I would major in, but taking pictures brought me joy, so I always signed up for classes. My senior year, things got weird." I swallowed past the lump in my throat.

"Go on," Fox urged softly.

"My teacher was nice. Always complimented my work and gave me after-hours access to the darkroom. It was during one of these times that he came on to me." Bile filled my mouth. "At the time, I thought I had imagined it, it was so swift, and he immediately gave me a project for the yearbook."

"But you didn't imagine it, did you?"

I shook my head. "No. The following days, he did more of the same. Compliment my work. Give me a special assignment, and then when no one else was around, touch me." My skin prickled, making me wish for a shower.

"How long did this go on?"

"A few weeks?" Why, oh why had I been so stupid? So gullible? "Then one day, he leaned in and started kissing me. I immediately shoved him away, but he accused me of playing hard to get. Even laughed." The words came fast, putrid-tasting as I remembered that day. "I fought back when he started kissing me again. Fought until he got the message and

I was able to run back to my door. Even though the bruises eventually faded, the scars remained." I covered my mouth. "Maybe I could have pushed the experience into the far recesses of my minds. Never revisited it. But once I became a model, I received more propositions than I could count."

The lewd come-ons and leering glances that made me feel as if I were being undressed always disgusted me and reminded me too keenly of my high school instructor. "I had a few who stole kisses, though no one else tried to rough me up. Still, every lustful comment and look only solidified my judgment of the male gender."

"Tori."

Fox had never said my name like that. Like he ached for me and hated that he couldn't keep the pain away. I took a chance and lifted my eyes. His voice had hinted at the sorrow, but his face showed pure agony.

"I told you I was a mess, Fox."

"Oh, baby, you're stronger than you realize." He knelt before me. "You're a warrior. You fought back and escaped."

"Then why do I feel so...so ashamed?" Hot tears continued to slip down my face.

Fox used his thumbs to wipe away my pain. "Because the enemy will use every trick to keep us in bondage. He's twisted your hurt to make you feel like you should have done something differently. Like you were in the wrong, and that is so not true. *He* was in the wrong. Your teacher took advantage of a *child*, someone in his protection. The shame is all his."

"Now do you see why we'd never work?" I searched his eyes, ready for him to agree. Steeling myself against his yes.

"Don't you know a man who works in security could only align himself with the strongest of women? That's you, Princess. And I want to be here when you slay every one of your dragons." He placed a soft kiss on my forehead, then stood, helping me up. "Go rest."

"That's all you have to say?"

"For now. When I show up tomorrow, and the next day, and so on, you'll understand I mean what I say. Hopefully then you'll trust me."

My chest heaved at the thought. That he could be trustworthy. That I could ever trust a man with my heart. I didn't know what to say, so I said the only thing that made sense. "Good night, Fox."

✻ 20 ✻

MY FINANCIAL WEALTH EXCEEDED HIS ABILITY TO COUNT IT, BUT my accountant liked to bug me with financial updates regardless. One of the first things he'd ever encouraged me to do was to give to charity. It seemed a little self-serving to give to charity and then receive a tax write-off, so I'd decided early on to offer my time as well, as a way to give back to the community. At least once a month I went to visit a local group home. The children there were all receiving medical treatment, but their illnesses didn't prevent them from sharing smiles and hugs. They were absolutely precious, and even though I was there to give to them, they were a balm to my soul.

Carly snuggled under my chin, her head resting against my chest, probably listening to my heartbeat. It's what she did every time I visited. The fourteen-month-old had lost her parents in the car accident responsible for the burns she was now recovering from. She was seen regularly at the burn center for the scars on her leg. I was still hoping a family out there would love on her and make her theirs.

Cuddling with Carly reminded me of a dream I'd once held. Of being a wife and a mother to as many kids as possible. The normalcy of the dream had gotten me through the loneliness of boarding school. But once modeling catapulted me into famed status, my dreams seemed foolish. How could I ask a man to build that kind of life with me?

Could I risk the paparazzi stalking my children the way Emmett and I had been targeted?

"I didn't know you liked children." Fox whispered so he wouldn't disturb Carly's snugglefest.

I peeked at him from beneath my lashes, careful not to move my chin and bump Carly's head. "What's not to like?"

"Kids are great. I just didn't think you'd agree."

There was a look in his eyes I was too afraid to explore. Yesterday's conversation still echoed in my brain when I wasn't actively trying to ignore the emotions Fox created. I could still feel the tenderness from his kiss at the fashion show. My whole body went tingly, and I glanced away, hoping he'd miss any telltale flush in my cheeks.

The punctuated sound of heels tapping on the floor out in the hall alerted us to an incoming visitor. Fox tensed. He rotated his shoulders and peered out into the corridor. His brow smoothed out, and he took up his position of half in/half out of the room once more.

When had I become so attuned to his movements? Was this what it was like? Falling for someone and letting them close? Having such an intimate knowledge of them that you knew what they were thinking without one word spoken? I wasn't sure what to think about romance beyond my fight or flight response kicking in and giving me an intense desire to flee. As soon as this stalker business was done, I was out of here. Maybe to spend my time lying on the beach and gazing at the ocean while eating local delicacies.

Leslie appeared a minute later wearing a child on her back like a koala. Her bright smile was as sunny as the freckles on her face and the blonde hair pulled into a high ponytail. "Hey, Tori, the girls were wondering if you could read to them."

"Of course." I rose and carried Carly to her crib, placing her down slowly so as to not wake her.

She sighed and popped a thumb in her mouth, turning onto her side but remaining in a deep sleep. The nursery room was my favorite, but I always made sure to spend time with the few preschool-aged girls as well.

"Are they in the playroom?"

"They are."

"Okay, thanks." I motioned for Fox to follow me as I left the nursery and headed for the staircase. The playroom upstairs was truly a marvel. The home received yearly donations that kept them in style. There were multiple play houses for the girls, a crafting area with tons of coloring books and art supplies, and the entire floor was covered in a rubber mat to pad the landing when the girls knocked into one another or tripped over their own two feet.

As Fox and I entered the space, Mandie spotted me first. "Princess Belle!" She clapped her hands and jumped up and down.

Soon the other girls followed her example, swarming me for hugs and calls to read a story. Fox quirked an eyebrow and murmured low, "And you had a problem with *me* calling you Princess."

I snorted. "They've seen *Beauty and the Beast* one too many times. What's your excuse?"

"I know nobility when I see it."

My heart skittered to a stop at the warmth in his voice and the admiration in his eyes. "I'm not noble," I whispered.

"Right, because donating your money *and* coming to visit is the most egotistical thing one can do."

"Fox, don't make me into someone I'm not."

"And don't ignore the virtues God gave you."

I swallowed. What was I supposed to say to that? He was intent on seeing me in a way that wasn't true.

Or is he really seeing the real you? The one no one gets to see?

Wanting to ignore those thoughts, I grabbed the nearest book off the bookshelf and settled onto the floor. The girls circled around me, some sitting crisscross applesauce and others lying on their stomachs. We'd done this so often they knew the drill.

As I read the story of *Goldilocks and the Three Bears*, my gaze shifted. Fox lowered himself to the floor in the back with a view of the exit. Before I knew it, Abigail had crawled over and curled into his side, and Jazz had laid her head on his free arm. My breath hitched. Suddenly, I could see us in a home together. Beautiful kids with his chocolate skin and my eyes, clamoring for our attention as we laughed over a shared joke.

The image was so sharp, so clear, I went mute. Couldn't see the words on the paper as my vision blurred.

"Pwincess Belle, are you sad?" Netta's big brown eyes took on a puppy dog quality.

I cleared my throat. "Sometimes I feel sorry for Goldilocks."

"Me too," Jenny chimed in. "She was all alone like us."

"Oh, not like you sweetie. You have Miss Leslie and you have me."

Jenny beamed, the gap between her two front teeth showcasing her adorable baby teeth.

"And Goldy has the bears," Abigail shouted from the back.

"She does." I nodded, glad they took my attention off my morose feelings.

"Who do you have Pwincess Belle?" Netta asked.

My stomach dropped to my toes. The questions kids came up with. Silence stretched as I scrambled for a response.

"She has me," Fox answered with confidence. "She also has some pretty great friends and family."

"I want a family," Jazz mumbled.

My heart broke for the little one. She'd been returned

multiple times to the home like she was some pet that hadn't worked out. It sickened me.

"You'll get one, Jazzy."

Her lips quirked in a half smile, as if she wanted to believe but couldn't quite bring herself to do so.

And wasn't that the same problem I had? I wanted to believe my past wouldn't prevent me from having a future, but I'd had such a hard time letting go that I couldn't see anything past it.

I swallowed and picked the story back up. It was time to give these girls a few minutes of contentment. Time to escape into a story where happy endings were assured and love could conquer all.

If only I could believe fiction could actually be reality.

Fox filled the living room. "We need to go—now."

"What's wrong?" I rose, sliding my feet into the shoes closest to me. Thankfully, the sandals went with my jeans, so I didn't look ridiculous.

How sad was it that my brain was focused on a potential disaster but still wondering what judgmental comments the public would make about my outfit when they caught me stepping out of the house?

"Ms. Ricci's been in an accident. She's alive but injured."

"What!" My heart jumped in my throat as I imagined all sorts of scenarios with Octavia front and center and not alive. *Calm down. Fox said she was alive.* "How bad is it?"

"Jax reported that the doctors haven't given an update."

I grabbed my phone and followed Fox to the car. My hands shook as I attempted to buckle in.

"Let me." Fox brushed my hands aside and clicked the seat belt. "She's going to be okay, Tori."

"You don't know that."

"Actually, I do. Jax has the situation under control. His voice was calm, which means she's fine, despite the lack of doctor communication."

"Was it the stalker?"

"I'll know more when we get to the hospital."

I nodded and stared unseeingly out the window. I'd thought this maniac would only target me. That's why I had Fox and an insane security system at home. How naïve, considering he'd possibly shot at Holiday already. Going into hiding wasn't keeping my roommates safe. Maybe I should announce over social media or in a press conference that I had a stalker and was done hiding.

"Talk to me. You're worrying me."

"I'm just thinking."

"That's a dangerous thing to do sometimes. I know you're scared."

"I'm petrified!" I gulped as the hot words erupted into the interior of his SUV. "What if we don't get him? What if he succeeds in killing someone I love?"

"We're going to get him, Tori. We're good at our job."

"But you're not superman. Or did you already forget about the gunshot wound and broken wrist?" Because I certainly hadn't. Could still picture how vulnerable he'd looked in the hospital and feel the guilt that clawed its way through my heart.

Another reason he needed to stay far away from me.

"I haven't forgotten. But if you'll remember, it was a graze, and the accident was just that—an *accident*."

I swung around at the anger in Fox's voice.

He flicked a signal on and pulled over. Cars whizzed by us.

"I won't let you run, and I refuse to let you push me away again." His hands held my chin gently in his fingers. "I will protect you with my last breath if I have to. You will be safe, and he'll be behind bars."

"I don't want you dying for me, Fox." The thought turned my heart to ice. "And how, *how* can you say I'll be safe when you can't see the future?"

"No, but I think we get glimpses sometimes."

I thought about the picture of us raising a family together. "I don't know."

"Tori."

He waited until I met his gaze. Strength poured from his dark eyes, and an intensity I'd never seen before captivated me.

"I've seen you in my dreams and felt a spiritual nudge for me to pay special attention. God doesn't grab people's attention for no good reason. He wants me to pay attention to *you*. I believe in His goodness and His desire to bless us."

"What are you trying to say?" And did I really want to hear it?

He lowered his head to mine. "I believe you're a part of His plan for me. And that certainty means everything will work out in the end. I don't know how yet, but I trust Him. Please trust Him with me."

I swallowed hard. "I don't know how."

His hands swallowed mine up. "Father God, I pray for Your divine wisdom to touch Tori's heart. To soften it and erode the unbelief wrapped around her. Please show her who You are and help her to trust in You completely. In Your Son's mighty name, amen." He placed a kiss on my forehead and pulled away.

I stared, flummoxed by what had just happened. Never had someone prayed for me in such a way. Without thought, I flung my arms around his neck and squeezed him tightly. "Why? Why would you pray for someone angry with God?"

Fox pulled back, his gaze intense. "Why wouldn't I? You believe in Him, and deep down you know He's good. If I can pray and help you see how much better your life is with Him leading it, then I will. Every day, forever and ever."

Maybe, just maybe, my future could be different. I could trust in a God who gave second chances. I could fall in love and trust this man with my innermost secrets and desires.

"We should go."

He nodded and put the car in drive, flicking his turn signal on.

"Will Emmett and Holiday be at the hospital?"

"Probably. Jax said he was calling them next."

"Oh good." I could use a hug from my friend and my brother.

In no time, we'd found a parking spot and joined Jax in the waiting room. He'd informed us Emmett and Holiday were on their way and that he still needed to hear from the doctor. Octavia had been taken to get some imaging done.

"What happened?" I asked.

"They were leaving the studio when a masked man made a grab for Octavia."

My heart leapt into my throat at the image.

"I went for him," Jax said. "and in the tussle, Octavia fell. She screamed in pain, grabbing her leg. That's why I brought her here."

How would she ever forgive me for something *my* stalker did?

Time passed as I sat in the corner of the waiting room with a cup of sludge they called coffee, just to give my hands something to focus on while I waited. The elevator chimed, and Holiday rushed out. I placed my cup on the end table, then jumped up, and raced toward her.

"Is she okay?" Holiday squeezed me tight then pulled away.

"We're still waiting. The nurse said the doctor would be out soon."

"How long ago was that?"

I checked the time on my cell. "Ten minutes?"

Holiday stepped aside, and Emmett wrapped me in his arms. "You okay, kid?"

"Freaked out," I whispered.

"We'll get this figured out."

"I hope so."

Emmett ushered Holiday and me toward the chairs. He sat down between us and I picked my coffee cup back up.

"How long have Fox and Jax been talking?" Holiday asked.

"Since we arrived."

"Do you know what happened?"

I relayed the details Jax had given me earlier.

"Do they think this is related to the stalker?" Emmett asked.

"They haven't said yet." But it had to be, right? What were the odds that all three of us would be targeted in such a short period of time? Sure, muggings happened, but the timing of this incident seemed a little too coincidental.

A doctor walked into the waiting room and we all stood. Jax and Fox stopped talking, turning to hear the doctor speak.

"I've treated Ms. Ricci, and she's given me permission to share an update regarding her health."

"Is she okay?" I stepped forward.

"Ms. Ricci has ruptured her ACL."

I swayed as his words sunk in.

"Oh, Lord, no," Holiday whispered.

Instinctively I threaded my fingers through hers. "What's her recovery going to be like?"

"She'll need surgery, however I don't have an opening until next month. She'll be released and need to start physical therapy to aid in her recovery. After surgery, the therapy will continue for several months."

"Will she be able to dance again?" Holiday asked.

My body tensed as I braced myself for his answer.

The doctor grimaced. "The likelihood of her continuing at her current level is slim."

Oh, Octavia.

"But not impossible?" Holiday asked.

"I don't want to make any guarantees. Let's just take it one step at a time."

"Can we see her?" Jax asked. "I'm sure Ms. Ricci would love her friends around her at this time."

"Of course. She said Ms. Brown and Ms. Bell could come back." He glanced at the iPad in his hand. "She's in room 4-220."

"Thank you." The words scratched my throat as emotions clogged my airway. How could I face Octavia knowing her career could be over because of me? I paused as Holiday started for Octavia's room.

Fox laid a hand on my arm. "It's not your fault."

"But…"

"Not your fault." He shook his head. "You didn't attack her."

His assurances did little to quell my guilt. "Do you think it was him?"

"Possible, but unless he sends us a letter saying so, it's just a guess. This could be purely coincidence."

That didn't make me feel any better.

"Go. She needs you."

"You're right." I straightened my shoulders and put on a brave face. Who knew what state Octavia would be in? Dancing was her everything.

If You care, please help.

❧ 22 ❧

OCTAVIA SAT IN HER HOSPITAL BED, A VACANT LOOK IN HER brown eyes.

"Tavia, oh my goodness, I'm so glad you're okay." Holiday flew to Tavia and wrapped her in a hug, burying her face in the curve of the ballerina's neck.

Former ballerina.

Holiday was wrong. Tavia was *not* okay. My heart shattered as tears welled in my eyes. *Don't cry. Be strong for her.*

Holiday stepped back, and I reached out to squeeze Octavia's hand. Her fingers were ice cold. "Do you need a blanket?"

She shook her head.

"Do you want me to call your folks?" Holiday asked.

I hid a grimace. I couldn't imagine the chaos of her parents descending on her. But at the same time, when your world had been shaken, didn't you need parental support?

Tavia shook her head again.

"Are you sure, Tavia?" I whispered.

She nodded. Still silent.

I exchanged a worried glance with Holiday. Was Tavia going to talk at all? Was she still in shock?

"The doctor said you'll have surgery in a month but to start physical therapy right away. I can help set that up." Tavia needed to know we were here for her. In any way she needed us.

She bobbed her head up once.

Unease slithered down my spine.

"Did they give you pain meds?" Holiday asked, her voice tight with concern.

"I don't know."

I closed my eyes in relief at the sound of Octavia's stark whisper just as the turmoil in her voice brought more tears to my eyes. "I'll go check." I flew out of the room, barely managing to close the door before a choked sob escaped past my lips.

"Princess, you all right?"

Fox's low tenor had me pulling my fingers apart, and I blinked at him past the curtain of my hands. The look of concern did me in. I flew into his arms, gripping his waist and silently crying into his chest while he rubbed soothing circles along my back.

"Just let it out," he murmured.

My tears flew freely until *finally* they subsided. I cupped my arms around Fox's back, placing my cheek against his heart. Heat radiated from his chest and warmed me to my core. But I couldn't sink into pity. Tavia need me.

I stepped back. "I probably look horrid," I sniffled.

"You always look beautiful. Never shy away from your emotions."

I met Fox's gaze, disbelief widening my eyes. "I *always* shy away from emotions. They're messy and get you into trouble."

"No, they tell you when you've truly loved. Anyone who's watched you three interact can see the love you have for one another."

Oh. I'd been thinking of a different type of love.

"Tori?" he whispered.

The door swung open, and I jolted away. Holiday's eyes widened to circles as her gaze darted from me and back to Fox.

"Uh, Tavia's asking for pain meds."

I nodded, wiping my face. "I needed a moment."

Holiday pulled a makeup wipe out of her clutch. "I don't blame you." She inched forward, leaning to whisper, "You so owe me a conversation about what I just interrupted."

"Not on your life," I whispered back.

"Oh, we'll see." She smirked. "I'll go find a nurse or doctor. And you, Tori girl, owe me a spa date soon."

I chuckled at her reference. When we'd gone to Napa Valley over the summer, we'd all spent time at a spa. Tavia and I had been convinced that Holiday liked my brother, despite her gross denial. Eventually she admitted her feelings, and now they were engaged. If she thought I'd spill about Fox, she had another thing coming.

Then again, she was my best friend. Maybe sharing about my inner turmoil would pull Tavia out of hers. I took another step away from Fox. "I'm going to go back in and make sure Octavia's all right."

"Understood. You good now?"

I nodded. "Thanks," I murmured.

"Anytime."

Octavia bored a hole in the wall with her intense stare. She didn't even blink when I crossed her path to come stand on the other side of her bed. I pulled up a chair and held onto her hand.

"I'm not sure what's going to happen, but we'll get through this."

"I'm nothing if I cannot dance," she whispered.

"That's not true. You have so much to offer besides dancing."

"Like what?" Her light brown eyes pierced me with the depths of her loss.

"Your heart. Tavia, you're the kindest person I know. The world needs more compassion, and you have it in spades."

"I need to dance."

"Then make sure to follow the physical therapist's recommendations."

"Why did God do this to me?"

I flinched, quickly trying to cover my reaction with one of sympathy. How could I answer that when even I struggled with wondering how a "good" God could let innocence be ruined and the perverted go free?

What do I say? What do I do to make this better for her?

I swallowed, mouth drier than the pavement on a New York summer's day. "God didn't do this." My words started out shaky, but I kept on talking. "That man in the mask, he's at fault. I have no idea why people like him are allowed to walk this earth and hurt others. It sickens me, breaks my heart. But what I do know is God is love." *He's Love.*

How could I forget the lessons they taught at the boarding school's church? How all-encompassing His love was? The words whispered in my heart, echoed true in my mind. "God is love, and that man who hurt you is not a part of God." Couldn't be if he'd hurt someone as precious as Tavia.

"Why did God let me get hurt then? He knows how important dancing is to me."

"I wish I knew. Wish I had some wise words to offer. I've battled with why injustice exists so often that, frankly, I'm tired of talking about it. But every single day you see examples of its perversion. All I can tell you is I'm here for you. Holiday is here for you. We'll get through this because we're overcomers. We can get through this. Together."

Tears splashed down Octavia's cheek. I stood and wrapped her in my arms as she clung tightly to me.

THE CAR RIDE BACK TO MISS ETTA'S HOME HAD BEEN QUIET. Thankfully, Fox hadn't tried to break it with trite platitudes. But he had offered the comfort of holding his hand. When we walked inside the apartment, Miss Etta sat in the living room, TV on mute and an open Bible in her lap. She peered at me and set her cup down.

"My poor dear. Fox told me about your friend." She drew me into her embrace, and I took care not to squeeze too hard. "I've been praying for you all."

"Thanks," I whispered. I drew away and looked over my shoulder at Fox.

"I'm going to go talk to Sasha." His steps retreated down the hall.

Miss Etta clutched my hand. "Now, what do you want to talk about?"

I sighed. "I'm not sure where to start." I sank into the couch cushions.

"Where the pain hurts the most."

"Octavia ruptured her ACL, and I can't help but feel like it's my fault."

"Did you physically assault her?"

"No, ma'am."

"Did you hire someone to do so?"

"No." My lips pursed at the point she was trying to make.

"Then it's not your fault."

"But if the stalker is trying to hurt those I love, then aren't I to blame?"

"No. We can't control another person's actions. We can only control ourselves."

And wasn't that the crux of it all? "Miss Etta?"

"Yes?"

"Why do you believe in a God that allows bad things to happen to good people? Innocent people?"

Surely Miss Etta would have a better answer than the one I gave Octavia.

"Because I don't measure God against those who choose to sin. Just like you wouldn't want me to judge you based off a few bad supermodels."

I jolted back. "Are you saying I'm judging Him unfairly?"

"Are you?"

My mouth dried. "But if He won't do something, who will?"

"Who said He wouldn't?" She shifted in her recliner. "Let me ask you a question."

"Okay." I eyed her warily. She looked like she had a few tricks up her sleeve.

"You've gone to church before?"

"Yes."

"What did you think?"

I thought back to the required attendance during my boarding school days. To the time Emmett had asked me to go. Honestly, I had liked what I heard each time. I just couldn't reconcile it with the hurt I saw in the world. I repeated my thoughts to Miss Etta.

"If you hadn't been hurt, if you hadn't seen heartache, do you think you would easily accept Him?"

"Yes." The words came swift and true.

"Do you blame Marcel for your friends being hurt?"

"What? *No.* He's done everything he can to ensure our safety."

"But your friend was still hurt. Your brother too."

"Not because of Fox."

Miss Etta arched an eyebrow. "Don't you see? Not just here"—she pointed to her head—"but here as well." She pointed to her heart. "God put rules in place. Then He sent His Son for payment of sins, leaving an open invitation to surrender and stop letting our flesh rule. He did *everything* He could to ensure we live a good, abundant life. But we still have sin, don't we?"

"Miss Etta..." I heaved a sigh. "I really hate that you're making a lot of sense right now."

She threw her head back with a laugh, slapping a hand on her thigh. "Oh, girl, I do like you. You've got grit and you've got heart. But you're also a little too stubborn." She wagged a finger at me. "You need to let that hurt go and surrender. He's waiting."

I HADN'T SLEPT A WINK. INSTEAD, THE BACK OF MY EYELIDS HAD become a green screen for vivid images of the heartache of Tavia's eyes. The bullet wound in Emmett's shoulder. The gunshot and broken wrist Fox had endured. McCall's panicked falsetto lent a bone-chilling audio to my imagination. Everyone was being targeted *but* me. Sequestering myself to Miss Etta's home hadn't kept my friends safe. It had only hurt them.

Tired of playing possum, I stuffed every article of clothing, every accessory, everything I'd brought along with me back into my duffle bag. Time for a plan. One that would hopefully put an end to this disaster. After writing a note to Miss Etta, thanking her for everything and placing it in her Bible, I called Special Agent Derek Jones and filled him in on my idea. He was a little apprehensive but finally agreed to it.

The cake tasting this morning would put everything into motion. Fox and I had been on the bakery's schedule for a week. Who would have thought the appointment would end up providing me the perfect opportunity to escape and put my future back into my own hands.

Fox would most likely be angry, but I couldn't let that

change my mind. I *would not* let another person I cared about get hurt.

I sat down on the chair in Sasha's bedroom and opened the Bible that always lay on her dresser. The edges of the pink cover were worn, as if she spent a lot of time between its pages. And surprisingly, I hoped she did. Hoped the evils of the world had left her unscarred.

Dumb. I shook my head. She'd lost her mother and was being raised by her grandmother. No one could escape the darkness completely.

I fingered the soft leather. Where should I start? Crease the spine and read whatever page the book fell open to?

I texted Holiday, hoping she was awake so early.

T: IF YOU WERE TO GIVE ME A VERSE IN THE BIBLE WHAT ONE WOULD YOU WANT ME TO READ?

H: EXODUS 14:14 IN THE NIV TRANSLATION.

A quick peek at the spine of Sasha's Bible showed I actually had that translation in my hand. I looked through the table of contents, searching for where Exodus started. After turning to the page and then searching for chapter fourteen, I found the verse Holiday gave me.

"The Lord will fight for you; you need only to be still."

Tears sprang to my eyes. Be still. Something I had so much trouble doing. I'd been so busy trying to fight my own battles and growing weary because of it. I didn't know how to be still. Didn't know how to let Him fight my battles.

God, what do You want from me? How can I just forgive those who hurt and go unpunished?

Let go.

The words were spoken in my mind as clear as day.

How do I just let go of the hurt?

Give it to me.

My breath shuddered. Holiday and Tavia had both urged me to talk to God. To tell Him how I felt, something I'd never done. I dragged in a deep breath and exhaled.

I'm angry. Angry that I never told anyone what he did to me. Angry that he has a chance to hurt someone else because I didn't speak out. Angry that the men I've run into seem to want only one thing. I turn on the TV and see injustice after injustice. People going free after killing a kid in cold blood. Every woman adding #metoo to her social media profile. Why, God? Why don't You just end it all?

A wisp of memory tugged at my consciousness, asking me to delve deeper. To remember what I'd been taught. The parable of the weeds. How a man planted weeds in the midst of wheat. But the man chose to wait until the time of harvest before separating the two.

Miss Etta's voice echoed in my mind. *"It's not time. Child, everything has its time."*

I didn't like what this world was turning into, but Miss Etta was right. It wasn't time to pull the weeds. God knew some of the wheat needed time to grow, to be given a chance to thrive before harvesting.

"Oh, God, thank You for pulling my blinders off," I whispered. I bowed my head, my lips moving in silence as I continued to pour out my heart. *Please help me figure out how to let go. How to forgive. How to trust in You. I'm so tired of being tired. So tired of guarding my heart from more hurt, only to continuously be attacked. And this stalker business, God, I'm so weary. Please help me to be still. To listen and heed as You fight my battles. Not me.*

It could no longer be *me*. I was done fighting. Round over, I was heading for the corner. To be still. To see how God chose to handle all that I could not change.

Chills erupted. *Please forgive me for all the times I've ignored You. For all the times I could hear You beckoning but turned a deaf ear. I'm so sorry.*

Forgiven.

NEVER IN A MILLION YEARS HAD I IMAGINED MYSELF AT A wedding cake tasting. The small rectangular offerings were enough for us to have an idea of how the dessert would taste but small enough to leave room for multiple samplings. I set my fork down, dabbing my mouth with a napkin. The strawberry champagne slice wasn't my favorite.

"Pass?" Fox asked.

"Definitely."

He chuckled. "Your nose crinkled with the first bite. I thought for sure you'd leave the rest on your plate."

"I don't want to be wasteful."

"That sounds like something Ms. Brown would say."

"Ha." Holiday would totally say that. She loved food almost as much as music.

"You don't seem to be a fan of the vanilla-based options, Ms. Bell." Jill, the baker, arched her brows, awaiting my reply.

"I do love chocolate."

"Be right back then."

Jill arrived with another tray, this time laden with chocolate decadence. She placed two plates in front of us. "This one is our chocolate with raspberry-cream filling. I noticed you both liked some of the cakes with fillings."

I shuddered, remembering how awful the lemon slice had been. Although, the raspberry did temper it. I took a bite and moaned in delight.

"Oh, this one is good," Fox mumbled.

"Agreed." I finished the cake, then took a sip of my ice water.

"I'm so glad you think so." Jill wrote on her notepad and placed two more dishes in front of us. "The next is our famous chocolate mousse. I've paired it with a buttercream frosting."

"Contender," Fox said after swallowing.

"I agree."

"Next up is German chocolate."

"Oh, pass." I waved my hand. "I forgot to mark coconut in the *I hate* column." I knew there was something I'd missed on Jill's questionnaire.

"But it's like a Mounds candy bar," Fox protested.

"Blech. Please don't ever eat that and expect a kiss from me." Heat immediately filled my neck and warmed my face. "Uh…"

Jill chuckled. "You guys are adorable."

Thank goodness she didn't catch my embarrassment.

"Okay, the last one is the coffee hazelnut cake. We usually do a fine layer of hazelnuts in the frosting. Some people pass on this option if they're expecting guests with nut allergies."

"No nut allergies on my side." I glanced at Fox. "You?"

"None."

"Fabulous." Jill beamed. "Try it."

I wanted to cry at the explosion of flavor that coated my tongue. It was like Nutella heaven and reminded me of the hazelnut bianco latte I drank. "This is perfect."

Jill shared a look with Fox.

"What?"

"Your fiancé thought you'd prefer this one."

My mouth dropped open as I stared at Fox. "When did you say something?"

"I called yesterday when confirming the appointment."

Even when we were faking that romantic feeling, Fox still looked out for me. How was I supposed to put my plan into motion when my heart wanted nothing more than to be tangled up in his?

I swallowed, overwhelmed. "Thank you."

"I'll give you two a minute." Jill grabbed the dishes and walked out.

Fox assessed me. "What's wrong?"

"I'm just amazed you knew which flavor I'd like the best."

"I know a lot of things about you."

My heart skipped a beat as my brain clued in. Was this the

reason Fox had studied me so intently since he'd been hired to protect me? What other things had he noticed? There was no way he could know what I planned to do. Yet it almost felt like he could read my mind like a Q&A article I'd interviewed for countless times before.

My plan was to fake a trip to the ladies' room and have Jill hand Fox a note detailing my next steps. He wouldn't be happy, and frankly, relying on the FBI had me on edge as well. But I was so tired of this uncertainty hanging over me.

It was now or never.

I turned to Fox with a pasted-on smile, the forced curve of my lips freezing.

Sweat beads dotted Fox's bald head, his face etched with a grimace.

I touched his arm. "What's wrong?"

"My stomach. I don't feel so—" He shot up and raced toward the back of the building, where the bathrooms were.

My eyes widened. Should I go after him? I worried my lip. Now would be an excellent opportunity to put my plan into action and walk out the doors to meet Special Agent Derek Jones.

"Tori, ma belle. What are you doing here?"

I whirled around. "Luc." I blinked. "What are *you* doing here?"

He stepped forward, eyes gleaming as he looked me up and down. There was a calmness about him that made my spine stiffen. He looked like the wolf who'd figured out how to get to the three little pigs. "I am here for you."

"What?" I stepped back, unease snaking its way through me. "Why?"

"Quite simple, ma belle. We belong together."

❧ 24 ❧

My heart thudded painfully in my chest, and I fought the urge to glance toward the bathrooms. "What did you do to Fox?" The words were like acid in my throat.

A delighted grin curled Luc's lip. "He'll be indisposed for a while. A few dollars, and the dishwasher was happy to slip something into the cake."

My stomach rolled. Poison? Would Fox be okay? I blinked. "But we both ate cake."

"Ah, but you do not like the coconut."

How did he *know* that?

He smiled. "Let's go, ma belle."

Fear stilled me.

But wait. The GPS tracker. Fox could track me, but would I be safe with Luc until Fox realized I'd been taken and could rescue me? I had no idea what Luc planned. What he'd do with me. Chills wracked my frame. "I thought we were friends." I gripped the back of the chair. "Why don't we sit and talk." I gestured toward the seating, hoping my voice sounded calm and reassuring.

Why had I insisted on a private tasting? If the storefront were full of people, Luc wouldn't be able to get away with this. There'd be witnesses. Someone who could help me. *Anyone.*

His brows dipped. "Non. We can talk in the car." He gripped my upper arm. "We are leaving now."

"But—"

He jerked me forward. "If you try to struggle, to alert anyone, I will detonate one of the bombs I've placed in areas that will cause your friends harm."

God? Please, no! I swayed. "All right. I'll come. Please don't hurt anyone else."

Luc trailed a finger down my cheek. "Good. You will see. All will be as it should be."

I turned to grab my clutch.

"Ma belle?"

"Yes?" I looked over my shoulder.

"Give it to me." He motioned for me to hand over my purse.

I passed it to him, and he opened it, rifling through the contents. Finally, he pulled out my burner phone. "This can stay. And leave your ring, too. You have no need of it."

Did he know? Surely not. I bit my lip, my fingers hovering over the beautiful ring. How would Fox find me if I left the jewel behind? *God, please be with me.* I gulped, sliding the ring off my finger and placing it on Fox's empty barstool next to the cell Luc had left there.

Jill entered from the kitchen area. "Oh, I didn't hear the bell. Can I help you with something, sir?"

My gaze flashed to Luc, and I shook my head in warning before turning to Jill with an Oscar-winning smile. "Jill, I forgot about my next appointment. Could you leave a message for my fiancé?"

"Of course."

I gathered all my strength to keep my voice steady and calm. "Tell *Marcel* that I went to get dressed for the fashion show." I wished I could ask her to repeat it verbatim, but I didn't dare.

"Certainly. Have a good day."

"You too."

Luc placed a hand on the small of my back, prodding me forward. A sleek sedan idled alongside the curb. He pressed a button on the key fob and then held the passenger door open for me.

"I can sit up front?"

"Ma belle, you are not my prisoner." He smiled, flicking his hair off his forehead. "You are *mon couer*."

Bile rose in the back of my throat. I didn't want to be his heart. Didn't want to be his anything. To think, all this time I'd counted him a friend. Without a word, I ducked my head and slid onto the leather seat. I stared out the window, willing Fox to come look for me. To keep me safe. Then I remembered the poison. The look on his face before he'd bolted to the restroom.

Would he even be able to get my message from Jill? *God, please keep him safe. Please don't let the poison be deadly. Please don't let Luc detonate any bombs.* I hoped Luc had been bluffing, but I didn't want to take any chances. *And please, let my clue be enough to tip him off about Luc.*

No way would my life skills be enough to escape from someone who had systematically found a way to get me alone.

Luc peeled away from the curb, throwing a smile my way. "Finally, ma belle, we are alone. Good, non?"

"Uh…" What should I say? "I had no idea how you felt about me, Luc."

"How could you not? All the time we spent together? My designs were created for you, ma belle. There is no one else."

My stomach sank. "But you never hinted. Never asked me out." *Like a* sane *person.* It wasn't as if I'd had a boyfriend the entire time I'd known him.

And just how crazy was he? He was acting like he was out for a Sunday drive instead of poisoning one person and kidnapping another.

"You were not ready. I could see these things." He tutted. "Imagine my surprise at the announcement of your engagement. I know you only wanted to make me jealous, because the Fox is not right for you."

But he is.

The force of my thought jolted me. Marcel Fox was perfect for me. He didn't want to change me. Only wanted me to have a life without walls so I would be able to have a fuller, richer existence. Everywhere I'd gone, Fox had been with me. Not solely for protection, but because he saw something in me that connected with him.

It was why he'd never been formal with me like he had with Holiday and Octavia. Even in the beginning, I'd gotten under his skin. Just like he'd gotten under mine.

But not in the way I'd first thought, like an irritant you couldn't wait to wash away. No...Fox and I were like a weaving of two into one.

I stifled a gasp with the realization. I wanted to be with Fox. Wanted to date and then experience all those firsts with him by my side forever.

What a time to get sappy and have a revelation.

Lord, could I have that dream? One of children and happily ever after with a man who adores me? Much like I saw my father and mother's mutual adoration that had led to thirty years and counting.

Luc took the next exit, and I frowned. "Where are we going?" His warehouse wasn't this way.

"Ah, ma belle, don't you know you belong with me? We are going to be married."

"What?" I gripped the door. "We can't get married!"

"Of course we can. That is what two do when in love. And New York"—he shrugged—"only has a 24-hour waiting period. We will get the license today and marry tomorrow evening."

No, no, no! I couldn't marry him. Was there a way a marriage under duress would be null and void?

"I'm engaged to Fox."

"No!" He slammed his hand on the center console. "You're not!" He flicked his hair back, as if trying to calm himself. "It was a ruse. I know this, my pet. You cannot fool Luc."

Obviously, bringing up Fox wasn't the way to go. I had to feed into his delusions. "Do we have everything to get a license? Do we have to do some kind of blood test?"

"No. Birth certificates and identification. That is all."

Oh, thank goodness. I didn't have my birth certificate. It was in a fire safe in my closet. "I just have my state ID."

"I have a friend who helped me." Holding the steering wheel with one hand, Luc opened the center console and pulled out what looked suspiciously like birth certificates.

The contents of my stomach rose unsteadily. "How?" I whispered. He wouldn't fake one, would he?

Luc smirked. "My associate retrieved it."

He'd been in my *house*! "Luc, what about my plans with…" I didn't say *his* name, hoping to keep Luc calm.

"Those plans, that is not you. A small wedding, bah!" He shook his head. "You were made for grandiose dreams, ma belle. You will have a wedding fit for a queen."

"But you said we're getting married tomorrow." It was impossible to put something together so fast.

"And we will." He stroked my arm. "I have been planning." He reached out, taking my cold hand in his. A light squeeze, and then his fingers began stroking the back of my hand.

I tried to keep the panic off my face, the disgust from curdling the cake I had so eagerly eaten with Fox. I couldn't marry Luc.

Think, Tor, think.

Trust Me.

The words pricked the back of my consciousness, reminding me of my conversation with God. *He* wanted to fight my battles. I only had to be still. I sank back into the leather seat.

God, please fight this battle and win.

❦ 25 ❦

AFTER DRIVING AN HOUR AND A HALF, LUC MADE A STOP AT THE local county clerk's office. He put the car in park and turned to look at me. "You understand we belong together, right, ma belle?"

I bit my lip and spoke cautiously. "No, I don't understand. You sent me threatening notes."

"Non, non." He made hushing noises, placing a clammy finger against my lip.

I fought off revulsion. His touch was *nothing* like Fox's.

"Those were to let you know we belong together. We were made for each other." He clasped my hand to his chest. "You must see."

"How can a dead rat prove that?" And the decapitated doll and other grotesque gifts he'd sent. Poor Holiday had been the one to open the package containing the rat. She still had Emmett opening mail for her.

He tutted. "My pet, you displeased me. You should not have gone to the FBI. Then you let your brother move in with you." He shook his head. "All of these things, they kept us apart longer than necessary. Don't you see?"

My mind whirled. I saw he was off his rocker, though I

couldn't point that little factoid out. Time for another tactic. "Luc, what if someone in the clerk's office recognizes me?"

"Then you tell them the *Enchantment* article was only a ruse. You wanted our love to be secret, non?"

No!

Don't set him off, Tor. I needed to keep him calm. Taking a deep breath in, I pushed out the words, "I can say that."

He beamed. "Ah, I knew it. We will be so happy together, ma belle. You will see."

"What about tonight?" I couldn't bear to even entertain what could be waiting for me and where. But I needed to know. Needed to be alert and think strategically.

"Ah, my associate has reserved a room for us at a hotel."

My throat tightened at the unspoken implication, then froze on a word Luc had said. "Your associate?"

"Oui. You did not think I would get my hands dirty, did you? I am a lover, ma belle. I could not shoot another person, kill a rat, or any of those other horrid things." He waved a hand in the air.

But he didn't have a problem hiring someone to do so? *Twisted.* I honestly had no words.

"Then you will come? Willingly? We must get the license." He gestured to the building.

What choice did I have? Besides, maybe someone in there could help me if I could get them alone. "I'll go."

"*Tres magnifique.*" He clapped his hands. "I will get your door."

The gentlemanly manners contradicted this whole ordeal. How could he threaten to kill the people I loved but insist on holding my car door open for me? I prayed for calm and a blank expression. If Luc knew how repulsed I was right now, well, I wasn't sure what he would do.

He placed his hands on the small of my back, guiding me toward the front doors.

This cannot be happening, God! Where is the cavalry? How long do I have to wait?

Because I wasn't sure how much longer I could fake a calm that had fled the moment I'd realized Luc was my stalker. My footsteps echoed on the tile floor as we followed the signs that read *marriage license.* This wasn't how I'd imagined getting married. In the deepest part of my mind, where I'd just barely allowed myself to begin dreaming, I'd pictured the small and intimate wedding Fox and I had been planning for. Having our friends and families there with the cathedral pointing like a beacon toward God.

Lord, I don't know how this can end well. I can't see past the panic making me sweat. I'm not even sure I know how to fully trust in You. If there was ever a time I needed justice, now's that time, God. Please. Please don't fail me. Please help me figure out how to trust. How to stay calm in this situation.

My words halted in my mind as Luc opened the door to the licensing office. A woman standing behind the counter smiled at us as we walked in. "Good afternoon, how can I help you today?"

"I started a marriage license process online," Luc stated, his hands positioned in a benediction. "We've come to finish."

"Wonderful. Congratulations." She offered him a smile before turning to me.

I froze, heartbeat pounding to a rhythm that matched the frenzied butterflies in my stomach. Her eyes roved over my face as if trying to catalogue my features or—dare I hope—recognize me. Because if she knew who I was, would she sense something was wrong?

Why didn't you alert the public to your stalker? Surely my fans and the world at large would have been all too happy to discover the culprit.

But I had thought keeping quiet the best. What happened to silence being golden?

The woman tilted her head. "Have either of you been married before?"

"No," we said in unison.

"Do you have your birth certificates and photo ID?"

Luc held up the documents, and I opened my purse to get my ID.

"Go down to booth number two, and I'll finish up the process with you." She pointed toward her left.

I searched for the numbers on the cubicle walls, then sat in the chair posed in front of her desk. Luc handed her the certificates and his ID. I swallowed, holding my hand out with mine. What would she say? Granted my ID had my full name—Astoria Lee Bell— not the nickname I was known for. But still, did this woman live under a rock? Fox and I had been on local news as well as worldwide entertainment news.

"Thank you, sir. Do you have the code from your online filing?"

Luc relayed the information, winking at her. If his idea was to be charming and not show the ugly underneath, then I had no hope this woman—her name tag said Amrita—would come to my aid.

"You do know you have to wait twenty-four hours, right?"

"Oui. Yes." Luc smiled.

She typed away on her keyboard, looking back and forth between the screen and our documents. She handed Luc his photo ID and then moved mine over. "Ms. Bell. Bell, Bell," she muttered before looking up. "Why does that sound familiar?"

I pasted on a fake smile. "I imagine Bell is a pretty common name."

"True. I feel like I just heard it though."

Just then, Whitney Houston's song "Run to You" came on. Wasn't that from *The Bodyguard* soundtrack? I couldn't decide if I should weep or laugh, so I bit the inside of my cheek to stop myself from doing either.

Amrita's gaze snapped to my face. "You're the supermodel," she gasped. "But"—she spared a glance at Luc—"he's not your fiancé." Her eyes dropped to my left hand, searching for the gorgeous ring I'd left behind.

I inhaled. "Some things in my life are publicity stunts." I held my breath, hoping I sounded sincere, praying Luc thought the answer satisfactory.

But while I waited for her response, I couldn't help but listen to the words of Whitney Houston. She was so right. If Fox walked in this door right now, I'd happily run to him, knowing he would do everything to protect me. Because he was good at his job, and because God had plans for us. I desperately wanted that to be true.

God, help me believe.

"Oh." Amrita deflated. "Well, congrats." At the sound of a printer turning on, she got up, retrieved a document, and handed it to Luc. "Where are you getting married?"

"At a nearby chateau."

"Oh." She breathed a sigh. "That's perfect." She turned to me. "I admit I liked the angle with the bodyguard, but everyone"—she blushed—"everyone knows Luc."

"You flatter me." Luc reached for her hand and kissed the back of her fingers.

"Oh no." She jerked it back, shooting an apologetic look at me. "I wasn't flirting."

"He's French." If there was a little extra snark, it had nothing to do with his nationality and everything to do with the hostage situation.

"Right." She gave a nod. "Have a great wedding day."

"We will." Luc bowed and then guided me out of the office and back to the imprisonment of his car.

LUC'S ASSOCIATE HAD BOOKED US A SUITE IN THE MOST EXPENSIVE hotel in South Salem. I'd had to fake a smile at the concierge and then at the receptionist who checked us in, all the while hoping someone would snap a picture and post it to social media. Surely Fox had people scouring every resource to find me. But everyone simply smiled and went about their business.

It was maddening! The *one* time I actually wanted someone to invade my privacy, was the time they chose to respect it.

I sat down in the suite's chair, swallowing a scream of frustration and clutching my purse as Luc sauntered over to the champagne bottle waiting in a bucket of ice.

He popped the cork and grinned at me. "We must toast."

Must we? The disgust that had been brewing in my stomach since Luc's appearance bubbled to the surface. Luc may be ecstatic to have me where he wanted me, but I was still praying Fox had recovered from the extra cake ingredient and was sending the cavalry my way. Surely a secret plan to track me had been in place. Right now, I wouldn't be mad if there turned out to be a hidden tracker sewn into my clutch or shoe.

Except Fox had always been respectful and courteous, telling me his plans and making sure I was okay with them. *Dang it.*

Luc handed me a flute of champagne. "To us, ma belle."

I forced my lips upward and tapped my glass against his. *To justice.* Because this time I wouldn't be silenced. The world would know what Luc had done to me. The nights I'd wakened from nightmares, imagining my friends dead. My own death. I would make sure he was put away for the maximum penalty.

And maybe I would even come clean about my high school experience. *The truth shall set you free* and all that.

"Drink up, ma belle."

I took a sip, holding it in my mouth. Was there a way to look like I was drinking but not? I wanted all my wits about me and didn't want the alcohol clouding my thinking. I stared down into the glass. What if he'd spiked it? Slipped a roofie in it.

Goosebumps erupted along my arms and a shiver had me wishing for a cardigan. *God, please don't let him hurt me.* Because, as much as I wanted to spit the champagne out, the intense scrutiny Luc aimed my way told me to swallow.

I took another sip for good measure, then set the glass on the end table.

"It won't happen, you know."

"What won't?" I eyed Luc, fighting to keep my lip from curling.

"No one is going to save you."

"You didn't set the bombs off, did you?" *God, please no.*

He waved a hand in the air. "I do not do things like that. That was merely a bluff."

My stomach dropped to my toes. "Then my friends are okay?"

"Of course, ma belle. I plan on inviting them to the wedding tomorrow."

What? Did he *not* think the cavalry would rush in as well? He must have seen the confusion covering my face, because he continued. "My associate will deliver the invitations tomorrow and inform them of the consequences if they alert law enforcement."

"Oh."

He guzzled the contents of his flute. "I knew you would want them there. Once we are married, the threats will cease."

I wanted to throw a hissy fit. I could *not* marry him. Not when my heart belonged to another. Why hadn't I taken the chances with Fox when he had offered them? I should have been braver.

"Before we arrived, I paid the hotel staff appropriately to ensure our privacy. Can't have your whereabouts on social media."

Way to burst all my hopes and dreams. I peered up at the ceiling to keep the tears at bay. "You thought of everything." My voice sounded oddly flat to my ears.

"Oui, ma belle. Our day will be perfect."

"And the chateau?"

"*C'est bon*! Wait until you see it. They have your dress waiting for you. Decorations. Food. Everything."

Dress? My stomach curdled at the thought. It was the one thing I hadn't searched for. The staff at the Loft Gardens had asked for our colors, which Fox and I had settled on during a mini powwow session, rose gold and ivory, and our menu preference. Yet the wedding and bridesmaids' gowns hadn't been determined. It was all fake, after all. But right now, I wished I'd looked so I wouldn't have to wear whatever design Luc had come up with.

I pressed my hand to my forehead.

"What is wrong?"

"Just a little tired." More like stressed to the max.

"Aw, you sleep. You'll see. In the morning, all will be as it should be, *n'est-ce pas*?" Luc held out a hand.

I didn't want to touch him, but I didn't know what he was capable of if I dissented. I placed my hand in his.

"Your room is there." He guided me over. "I will be over there." He pointed to the opposite room. "Please, let me know if you need anything. Anything at all. It is yours."

I searched his eyes, seeing sincerity but also something I'd never detected before. Luc was unhinged by his delusions. How had I never noticed? Why was I such a bad judge of character?

"Sleep well, ma belle."

I dipped my head in acknowledgement and opened my door. Tears of relief welled in my eyes when I closed the door and saw it had a lock. I pressed my ear against the wood, listening to hear if Luc moved away. I didn't want him to hear the lock click. The pressure in my chest eased a little as soon as I secured the door.

I raced across the room and quietly lifted the hotel phone off the hook. Nothing. How had he managed that? I sank to the floor, pressing the heels of my hands to my eyes, tears streaking down my face. I held the sobs in, keeping quiet on the outside, but on the inside, I screamed to the only One who could hear me.

God, please help!

Miss Etta's voice echoed in my mind. *"But You, O Lord, are a shield for me, My glory and the One who lifts up my head."* She told me I would never be defenseless. That God was my shield. How I wanted to believe that so badly.

"Okay," I whispered. "Look on the bright side."

Looking for the good wasn't something I usually did. Pointing out every flaw: check. Ignoring the positives: double check. But right now, I needed to calm my mind and hold onto hope, no matter what my current situation looked like.

1. Luc hadn't hurt me.
2. I had a locked door between my captor and me.
3. There were no bombs.
4. God was my shield and told me to trust Him.

I didn't know what would happen, but I had to hold onto hope. Because without it, I was a sitting duck.

❧ 27 ❧

MORNING CAME TOO SOON. I SAT UP IN THE BED, LOOKING AT THE barricaded door. I had moved all the furniture I was capable of pushing in front of it last night before falling into a fitful sleep. I walked over, climbed onto the desk, and put my ear against the door, listening.

Whispered conversation greeted me. Was Luc's henchman here? Should I open the door and see who it was? I bit my lip and began to move everything away from the frame. A quick listen told me they were still out there. I quietly turned the knob to unsecure the lock. Drawing a breath, I cracked the door just a bit.

My eyes about popped out of my head. *He* was the associate? I quickly locked myself in once more. My heart pounded furiously, and I became lightheaded. I sank onto a chair I'd dragged over.

Oh, God, I was not expecting him in a million years. Please, keep me safe.

Because I had no doubt that man was here for revenge. Pure and simple.

A knock reverberated through the room, and I jumped, heart leaping. "Yes?" I croaked.

"Ma belle, breakfast. You are hungry, non?"

No. I wouldn't be hungry for a long time. "I'm too anxious." *Please buy that.*

"Join me anyway. You do not have to eat, but I wish to see your beautiful face."

I stuck my finger in my mouth. *Gag!* "I think I should get more rest."

"No."

The deadly quiet tone passed through the door a lot more sinisterly than I'd imagined. I gulped, staring down at the lock. How easy would it be for him to get in? Why had I never taken defense classes?

The doorknob rattled. "Open this now."

"I need to use the restroom."

"You have two minutes, then my associate will break in."

I swallowed—a difficult feat with my tongue stuck to the roof of my mouth. I quickly used the restroom, washing my hands and eyeing the door. A knock sounded.

"I'm coming."

"Good."

I said a prayer and opened the door. Luc smiled, his grin stretching across his face. He fluttered his hair back and gestured for me to come out.

"We have the best breakfast. Croissants, strawberries, and more."

"Maybe I'll just have some coffee."

His nose wrinkled. "They did provide a carafe, but wouldn't you like to try tea instead?"

Was I dead? No way I wanted to drink dirty leaf water. I didn't know how tea drinkers downed the stuff. "I'll pass."

"Ah, we were bound to have some differences."

Where had his *associate* gone? A discreet look around the suite proved us alone. I sat at the dining table and poured myself a cup of coffee. "Is it just us? I thought I heard another voice." I tried for an innocent look.

Luc dabbed at his mouth. "It is. My associate has left to see to other business."

"What other business?"

"He will deliver the invitations and ensure the chateau is as it should be."

What was his obsession with things being as they should be? That tipped way past neurotic. I'd always known he was fastidious in his fashion creations, but I'd had no idea he was this obsessive. Could I exploit this knowledge in some way?

Luc continued eating, taking breaks in between bites to spin the delusional tale of our perfect day. How there would be a string quartet. Champagne. Appetizers. A seven-tier strawberry-champagne flavored cake. White lilies covering the venue.

All I could think was *not me, not my wedding*. Not without Fox.

I kept silent while Luc continued to monologue about his deluded ideas of marriage. Did he seriously think I would say yes? Now that I knew the threats were empty, there was no reason to stay. Except I wasn't sure what would happen if I attempted to walk out of this room. I certainly wasn't going to ask him.

"What happens after the wedding?" I looked into Luc's eyes, wanting the truth. The real truth, not one that existed only in his mind.

"A honeymoon, of course. I thought you'd like to visit my hometown."

"You want to go to France?"

"Oui, ma belle. You must meet my family. They could not be here for the wedding. And then you will see where I grew up."

My head dropped to my hand. "Luc, I…"

"What is it?"

"You don't want to marry me. You don't *know* me."

His lip curled. "And you think that plebeian does? I have

watched you. Been to every runway show. I have all the magazines you've been featured in. I *know* you."

No. He knew the façade I wanted the world to see. Only Fox had ever tried to break through my barriers. To not assume that what I projected was what went on in my head.

"You don't," I whispered. I hadn't really understood myself until recently. So how could a few magazine photos and runway shows tell the whole picture?

"Don't speak like that, ma belle." Luc laid a hand over mine. "I am sure you must be a little leery. But I only want the best for you, and that is *me*. No one can love you like I do. You will see. Time will show."

"Can I leave?" I pointed toward the door. My finger shook, and my mind screamed for me to take the question back.

"Why do you want to leave? Are you ready to go to the chateau already? See your dress?"

No, no, no. I wanted to go back home. To my friends. To Fox. I wanted this nightmare to be over.

God, please fight my battles.

Luc stood. "Come. You will see it is perfect."

I stood, my stomach in knots, but I was also a little relieved he hadn't flipped a lid at my question.

"You will come willingly?"

"If I say no?" *Tori, think before you speak!*

A frown marred his brow. "I do not wish to have to subdue you, but I will. My associate left me with some tools to aid me if you do not wish to see reason."

I just bet he did. "Fine." I grabbed my purse and walked out of our suite.

As Luc drove us from the hotel to the chateau, my mind repeated the litany *God, fight my battles.* Every time I thought I could escape, or at least walk away, Luc proved he had something up his sleeve. I would almost rather he'd hit me or beaten me. Then maybe I'd feel like a genuine hostage instead of a person making the choices.

How sick was that?

A castle-like structure rose in my view. Any other day, I'd admire the brick structure dotting the green landscape, but now it just represented my doom. Luc parked and held the door open for me.

"You are going to love the dress. I went with a ball gown style. Scoop neckline and delicate beading on the entire gown. It is a dream."

And nothing like I'd pick. I'd been crammed into so many bridal gowns for photo shoots that were over the top. Fox and I had wanted simple.

Tears pricked my eyes. Why couldn't I get the details out of my head? What Fox and I had, well, our plans were all fake. But those feelings running in my heart, filling my being, were very much real.

I would have picked a heavier weighted silk, maybe one that followed my curves with only buttons as an ornamentation. No excessive beading, lace, or any of those things. I'd done that. Played the bride. I wanted something different for my actual wedding.

I followed Luc until I stood in front of the wedding dress he'd designed. He checked his watch. "It is almost time for the festivities. I will send someone in to do your hair and makeup, and then my associate will walk you down the aisle."

My stomach dipped. I'd always pictured my father walking me down the aisle on my wedding day. Sadness pricked at me until I realized this wasn't real. None of it. No way would I want my family to participate in some delusion Luc had cooked up in his mind.

"Fine."

"It will be as it should be. You will see."

❧ 28 ❧

I TOOK A DEEP BREATH AS I STOOD BEFORE THE DOOR OF THE bridal chamber, knowing the time had come. The ladies who had been hired to help me had left, tittering about the romance of it all. I'd asked to use one of their cell phones when they were helping me dress. To my dismay, I found out Luc had confiscated them from all the working staff. Once I was dressed, Luc's henchman had taken up space in the corner of the room until they were done.

Now he'd returned. I twisted the handle and saw Jack standing there. His blonde hair was gray at the temples and his blue eyes looked cold as ice.

He leered. "Tori."

I tried to swallow, but my mouth was dry. "So, you're Luc's partner."

"He has something I want." He trailed a finger down my arm.

Acid churned in my stomach as I faced the man who tried to rape me at sixteen. *You're not sixteen anymore.* I shifted backward. "Why are you helping him?"

"Come on, don't be like that, Tori. We could have a great time. What Luc doesn't know won't hurt him."

His hot breath stung my nose as powerfully as his insinuations stung my sensibility. Before I could register movement, my hand connected to the side of his face.

"You—" He cut off an oath as his hand gripped my arm, squeezing with all his strength.

I cried out and my vision wavered.

"You are at my mercy." The words pierced through his gritted teeth.

I tried to ignore the pain in my arm. "But I don't think Luc would appreciate your actions." At least, I hoped that threat was enough to get Jack to back down. What twisted world did I live in where I was appealing to my assailant by bringing up my stalker? It was enough to make my head spin. But whatever got him to stop looking at me like he was a starving man and I was his last meal.

Jack gave a derisive snort. "Luc has a few screws loose. He believes you'll fall madly in love with him."

"And you?"

"I want what you denied me the first time. I know you told."

The words were like ice. "What are you talking about?"

An ash-blond eyebrow rose. "Why do you think I got fired? Brent told the administration because you told Brent."

I'd never spoken two words to Brent. He'd been too shy to do anything but stare at me. And considering the creepy way my *teacher* had been, I'd ignored all his looks. Had Brent seen what happened? "I never said a word." My words whispered in the air.

Jack cursed. "He must have been following you."

"He didn't reveal my name?" Because not a single person in the administration had ever asked if I'd been assaulted.

"I guess not." He looked at me. "I thought you told."

I shook my head, wishing he'd loosen his grip. "But are you really surprised someone found out how disgusting you are?"

He smirked. "Please. You were coming on to me. I can read between the lines."

I hated that his accusations were finding a slippery slope in my mind. *No.* I hadn't done anything to deserve his unwanted hands on my body. I wanted to believe that, but hadn't I wondered if I'd caused the assault? If I'd inadvertently done something that made him think I wanted *that*?

I straightened my shoulders. "No. I was a child. *You* were the adult."

"And now look who's all grown up." He gave me a heavy-lidded gaze.

Bile puffed out my cheeks. "Why? Just why would you help Luc?"

"You deserve every heartache. I'm only sorry I didn't take out your brother and Ms. Brown together."

I gasped at the cruelty in his cold eyes. "You attacked Octavia." It was more statement than question. Luc had already said Jack had done all the dirty work. But I needed him to say it.

Jack loosened his grip and slid his hand down my arm. "She'll live, so what does it matter?"

His words were a punch to my gut. "She may never dance again."

A cruel smile lit his face. "Is that right? Personally, I'm hoping Luc lets me have a go of it." He chucked me under my chin.

My mouth dried. "Did he promise you that?"

"Of course not." Jack snorted. "He's too *in love* with you. But what he doesn't know..." His voice trailed off as he took a step closer.

"I fought you off once, I'll do it again."

"Ah, but you forget. I'm the one who does all the dirty work. You won't get away from me this time."

God, help me. Because what he said was true. Sure, I could take another swipe at him, take off running, but being weighed down by an enormous ball gown wouldn't have me beating any sprinting records.

"Ah, there you are."

Jack turned toward the wedding coordinator coming down the walkway. I prayed he wouldn't hurt her.

"Your fiancé is rather impatient and sent me to find you. They're ready to start."

"Oh, okay." My pulse went into triple time. Were Holiday and Octavia here? Had they brought help?

Jack hooked his elbow out for me to slide my arm through his. "There will be a next time," he threatened.

It pained me to be this close to him, to fake propriety, but I had no plan. I only knew God wanted to fight my battles. And if ever I needed Him to do so, today was the day.

We walked behind the coordinator who disappeared to the side when we arrived at the gardens behind the chateau. The "Wedding March" started, and I slowly strode down the aisle. There in the audience were Octavia and Holiday. My throat squeezed tight. The only other people attending were Luc's assistant, but I saw a camera set up, its red light blinking. Was he streaming this or simply recording it?

Holiday's eyes widened when she caught sight of Jack, and her gaze slid to me, scanning for any injuries. She placed a hand over her mouth, but I saw the fire in her eyes. Octavia had tears in her eyes as well. *It will be okay* she mouthed.

I tucked my chin just a bit for her to know I understood. Hopefully, this would all be over soon—a nightmare I could actually wake from. Seeing my girls gave me the strength to continue walking. To continue hoping that God would bring me justice.

Jack delivered me to Luc, who winked as if this were an ordinary day. The officiant began speaking, and disappointment filled me. I'd been sure Fox would have some plan to rescue me, but with only Holiday and Octavia sitting on my side of the aisle, my hope filtered out.

God?

The officiant cleared his throat and spoke in a booming voice. "If anyone objects to this union, speak now or forever hold your peace."

My eyes widened and latched onto Luc, who discreetly shook his head. My lips parted. Dare I?

"I object."

Relief flooded my body at the sound of Fox's voice. I whirled around and tears sprang to my eyes as he marched down the aisle. The sound of a revolver cocking echoed in the shocked silence. My eyes widened as Jack pointed a gun at Fox.

"Don't take another step."

Luc leaned in. "Always have a backup plan."

I shoved the heel of my palm straight out and slammed into his nose. Wrestling sounded behind me and shouts erupted. Luc grabbed his nose and dropped to his knees. The officiant fainted, landing flat on his back. I turned to see if Fox had everything else under control.

Jack was on his knee, being cuffed by Jax—hello! Where had he come from?—and Fox rushed to my side. He wrapped me in his arms, squeezing me close to him. The tears I'd held back flowed freely as I buried my face into his chest.

"Did he hurt you?" Fox whispered in my ear.

"No," I croaked.

"Are you sure?"

I bobbed my head up, tightening my grip.

"Everything's okay. He can't hurt you any longer."

I pulled back. "Jack." I pointed a shake finger. "He did everything Luc asked, and he's the one…" My voice faltered as I met Fox's concerned gaze. "He's the one who attacked me in high school."

Rage darkened Fox's eyes and his jaw ticked, but the gentle hand that cradled my face did me in. I sobbed and let lose all the turmoil I'd bottled up since Luc had walked into the cake tasting yesterday.

I had so many questions, but they could wait. Because right now, I needed the safety Fox was offering me. And I'd never felt as safe as I did in his arms.

❧ 29 ❧

TEARS SLIPPED DOWN MY CHEEK AS I STEPPED INTO MY BEDROOM.

After hours upon hours of speaking to the FBI and local law enforcement, I was finally home. And though I hadn't wanted to be apart from Fox, I desperately needed space to recharge. To find some kind of normalcy.

I shuffled to my closet and pulled down the weighted blanket. If ever I'd needed the comfort of a hug, tonight was the night. I slipped into pajamas then slid into my crisp clean sheets. A sigh escaped as my own bed—which I'd missed these past few weeks—cushioned my weight. I pulled the weighted blanket up to my chin and exhaled.

Why? Why had I had to go through that? Endure Luc's insanity and Jack's lecherous behavior?

God was quiet, but I didn't feel slighted or forgotten. I imagined Him by my side, watching over me as I sought comfort from my things. From my room. My own home. Maybe His presence was even in the weighted blanket, wrapping me in a hug that would be a balm to my soul and healing to my internal wounds.

Thank You for saving me. For returning me home.

I wasn't sure what to do now. What my life would look

like going forward. Should I cancel every couples outing Fox and I had agreed to? Or go back to the way things were before the threats and fake engagement? Now that Luc and Jack had been arrested, for all intents and purposes, I could return to normal. But I couldn't seem to remember what normal looked like. Maybe I should continue staring at my ceiling and letting my thoughts spin faster than the fan's blades churning the air.

"TORI?" A VOICE PUNCTURED MY DREAMS.

I rubbed my eyes, glancing at the clock then eyeing my door. My pulse picked up speed as memories warred with the present. I staggered toward the door. Opening it a crack, relief filled me at the sight of my friends. "Hey, come on in."

Holiday trailed behind me as Octavia limped behind her.

"Oh good, you're awake." Holiday stood at the foot of my bed. "How are you feeling?"

I stared at my best friends, wondering why they were acting so reserved. "What's wrong? Is it Fox? Jax?"

"No, no." Octavia held up a hand. "Everyone is fine. It's *you* we're concerned about."

"Why? I told you Luc didn't hurt me."

"Sweetie, it's one o'clock," Holiday responded.

I looked to the alarm clock on my nightstand, registering the little p in the bottom corner. "In the afternoon?"

They nodded.

"I just woke up."

"Are you sure you're okay?" Holiday's brows looked like earth worms trying to figure out which direction to go. "You wouldn't tell us what happened. And you've been asleep forever."

"Is that why you guys haven't hugged me?"

"I didn't know if he..." Octavia licked her lips. "We didn't want to touch you if he'd...you know."

I sighed. "He didn't. Please give me a hug and stop giving me a complex."

Octavia giggled and Holiday ran to my side and wrapped her arms around me. I laid my head on her shoulder, tears appearing once more. How could I keep on crying? I was going to end up in the hospital from dehydration.

The bed shifted, and Octavia joined in the group hug. Calm slowly filled me as the realization sank in. I really was home. It was over. I didn't have to worry anymore.

I just didn't know how to still my thoughts in the wake of the past month.

"I was so scared for you," Tavia whispered. "When he showed up with the wedding invitation, I was appalled."

"Ugh." Holiday pulled back. "If I could have clawed his eyes out, I would have. But we knew we had to be smart about it."

I wiped my face with my night shirt. "How did you tell Fox? Luc said Jack was prepared to silence you if necessary."

"Fox had been camped out in the guest room since he informed us what happened at the cake tasting. Emmett called a doctor to make sure Fox didn't have any lasting complications. And thankfully, the doctor gave him a clean bill of health and told him to hydrate. Fox thought there would be a ransom note, so it was easy to tell him about the wedding."

"And since he was already in the house..."

"It looked like we didn't alert anyone."

"Thank goodness." I sighed.

"Fox called the police and they put plainclothes men at the chateau so they would be present to put a stop to it all," Octavia said.

"Good thing, too, because Luc was confiscating all cell phones."

"My heart about dropped to my toes when I didn't recognize anyone from the security team." Oh, how I had searched for a sign of anyone from Fox's team.

"I would have signaled you if I could've," Holiday said. "But Fox told us to act normal."

"My stomach felt like we were on a boat." Octavia placed a hand against her abdomen. "I never want you in that situation again. Maybe we should have security nonstop."

I blanched. As much as I had come to appreciate Fox protecting me, the idea of losing the freedom of privacy chafed. "I don't know how I feel about it all. My emotions are all over the place." I stared down at the comforter. "How am I supposed to act now? What's my new normal?"

Holiday squeezed my arm. "We'll figure it out together."

"And maybe Fox would like to help you with that?" Tavia suggested softly.

Could that vision of him and me with a house full of kids be closer to reality than I realized? "Maybe," I whispered.

"How about we have that spa day?" Holiday suggested.

"Yes, please. That sounds wonderful." I gave her a smile—well, as much as I was able. I still felt off, but if doing something "normal" would help right me, I'd do it.

God, please let it be so.

THE NEXT MORNING, I WOKE LESS CONFLICTED THAN THE DAY before. The spa day had helped me shed some of my confusing emotions, but now, as I studied my work calendar, I could feel some of the uncertainty coming back. Fox and I were supposed to go to an art showing tonight. It was one of the events McCall had thought would help establish us as a legitimate couple.

The news had been all over my harrowing almost-wedding, and I'd had to silence my phone. Dad had contacted our publicist to release a statement. Maybe I could get his opinion on what to do about my fake engagement with Fox. The logical direction would be to come clean and tell the world why he'd posed as my fiancé. But the mere thought filled me with dread. His text yesterday had informed me he'd be spending time tying up loose ends before he could come by, but I hadn't responded. What could I possibly say when I didn't understand my own emotions?

I sighed and called for a car service, then texted Dad.

T: ARE YOU AVAILABLE FOR BREAKFAST?

D: FOR MY FAVORITE GIRL, ALWAYS.

I rolled my eyes.

T: I'M PRETTY SURE MOM'S YOUR FAVORITE.

D: NAH, IT'S BEEN YOU SINCE YOU FIRST WRAPPED YOUR TINY HAND AROUND MY FINGER. DON'T TELL YOUR MOTHER.

I chuckled. I loved my parents.

D: DO YOU WANT ME TO SEND SECURITY AND A CAR?

T: NO. I ALREADY REQUESTED CAR SERVICE. THE THREAT IS OVER SO SECURITY ISN'T NECESSARY.

D: WE'LL TALK MORE WHEN YOU GET HERE.

I pursed my lips. That meant my father wanted me to have a detail a little longer. Probably more for his peace of mind than mine. I quickly dressed in skinny jeans, a teal silk tank top, and added a chocolate-colored blazer to complete my look. Just because I'd been a hostage a few days before didn't mean the media would forgive me for looking haggard.

Moments later, I found myself in the backseat of the Town Car and on my way to see my parents. The city sights sped past as Mac turned here and there. I sighed, resting my head against the headrest. It was so comforting knowing no one would shoot at me once I got to my destination. But it was also terribly quiet. I missed the banter that was always there between Fox and me.

Soon, the car slowed and pulled in front of the hotel where my folks were staying. Mac turned and looked at me over his shoulder. "I'll get the door. Just sit tight."

"Thanks, Mac."

He got out of the car, and a moment later my door opened. I frowned. No way he'd gotten to my side that quickly. I froze, but relaxed when a familiar hand offered assistance. I looked up and into Fox's handsome face.

I hadn't focused on my feelings where he was concerned, but now that I had the time to study his smiling face, it hit me. *He* was home. Fox was who centered me and brought a rightness to my life. I placed my hand in his and thanked God for the clarity.

❧ 30 ❧

Fox pulled me closer. "Are you avoiding me, Princess?"

My eyes widened. "What?" I'd spent too much time wondering what I would say once we finally spoke again. I just hadn't imagined it would be in front of the Waldorf Astoria.

"How come you haven't called me back?" His arched eyebrow might as well have tapped impatiently.

"I'm so sorry. I turned off my phone earlier. Too many reporters."

Relief filled his eyes. "I didn't even think about that."

"They're rabid when a new story breaks."

He chuckled and scanned the area. "I think we should finish this inside."

I tensed, resisting the urge to examine my surroundings. "Did you see something?"

"No." He shook his head, and a small smile lifted the corner of his mouth. "I just don't want to give anyone a photo op."

"Oh. Right." My shoulders sagged.

Fox threaded his fingers through mine and tugged me gently toward the entrance. I couldn't help glancing at him in

185

my periphery. What did it mean that he was here? Still calling me Princess. Holding my hand. Was it all to keep up appearances or did his actions mean more?

When I show up tomorrow and the next day and so on, you'll understand I mean what I say. Hopefully then you'll trust me.

My heart warmed as I remembered Fox's words. Was this him showing up? Proving he wanted a relationship beyond the one we'd created for public viewing?

As we stepped into the lobby, Fox pulled me toward a corner.

"Where are we going?"

"Somewhere private." He turned down a hall and looked up and down it before stopping. He placed his hands on my shoulders then slid them down to cup my elbows. "How are you?"

"Disoriented." I shrugged. "That's about the only way I can think to describe this jumbled mess inside of me."

"Your body has to catch up and realize you're not in danger anymore."

"I'm not really sure how to do that."

He smiled softly. "I'll help."

"Will you?" I bit my lip, hating the vulnerability in my tone.

"Of course I will." He cupped my face with both hands. "I'm in this, Tori. I'm not going anywhere."

Tears filled my vision and I swiped them away. The steadiness that Fox exuded wasn't just a balm to my soul. His warmth filled my heart with a rightness. Like my soul knew he was it for me. I exhaled out my emotions. "I love you, and I'm so sorry I didn't tell you sooner."

Fox's eyes widened before a stunning grin parted his full lips. He inched closer. "Do you now?"

"Fox…" I shoved his shoulder.

"First you tell me you love me, and now you're pushing at

me. Always making things complicated, aren't you, Princess?"

My lips twitched as I fought to hold in my laughter. "That's not how I imagined this going."

"How about this." He stepped so close, our shoes touched. "Tori Bell, I love you to distraction. And I want to show you every single day my body draws breath just how much you mean to me."

"You're going to make me cry."

He dropped his forehead to mine. "And you're going to undo me."

I wrapped my arms around his neck, loving the cocoon we'd created between us. "I thought about you."

"When?" he whispered, matching my tone.

"When Luc had me. I kept asking God to fight my battles and picturing you as the warrior He sent to keep me safe."

"Oh love, I want nothing more than to slay your dragons."

I chuckled. "You've gone completely sappy. I love it."

"And I love you." His hand cradled the nape of my neck and then his lips touched mine.

It was nothing like that time at the fashion show, because now I knew I was loved. Knew Fox cherished me and would fight for me, for us. He deepened the kiss, and I matched his fervency.

Someone cleared their throat. Fox pulled back and we both turned toward the noise.

My neck heated with mortification. "Hi, Dad."

"I was wondering what had happened to you until someone sitting in the lobby mentioned you'd gone this way."

"Uh, Fox and I were just talking."

"R-ight." Dad smirked. "That's what you're calling it these days?"

Parents. Only they knew the ultimate way to humiliate a person.

Dad clapped his hands together. "If you can pull yourself away from one another, your mother has brunch waiting in our suite."

"Thank you, sir," Fox said after stepping away. Thankfully, he reached for my hand, because I wasn't ready to sever contact yet.

We followed my father until we entered his hotel room. For a moment, my body broke out in a sweat as I remembered the suite in which I'd slept in—door barricaded, afraid Luc would break through.

My mom wrapped her arms around me, grounded me in the present. "Oh baby, I'm so glad you're okay."

I snuggled into her embrace. "I love you, Mom."

"I love you too, Astoria." She pulled back, searching my face. Probably using her motherly intuition to see if I was truly okay. She tapped my lips. "Someone's been busy with extracurricular activities."

"Mom!" I stepped back, trying to keep my hands by my side and not on my cheeks.

"Oh, hush. We know you two are in love." She waggled her fingers at us. "Come, let's eat."

I shook my head and followed them to the dining table. A nice variety of fresh fruits and pastries had been laid out along with breakfast meat and eggs. My stomach grumbled at the smell of bacon. One of the best smells, second to coffee.

Dad placed a Starbucks cup in front of me. "I got your favorite."

I took a sip and sighed with pleasure. "Thank you so much, Dad." None of that stuff Luc had tried to foist off on me.

My father said grace, and soon we were eating. After several moments of silence, he dabbed his mouth and looked at Fox. "I can't thank you enough for keeping our girl safe."

"It was my pleasure." Fox winked at me.

"We want to give you a token of our appreciation."

One of my eyebrows hiked upward. This was news to me. "What were you thinking?"

"Well, your mother and I were talking about it all last night, trying to figure out what to do."

"And? What did you come up with?" My gaze darted between Mom and Dad.

"We decided," Mom began, looking at Dad before settling her gaze back onto Fox, "to leave it open. As much as we wanted to pick something special and meaningful, we don't know you all that well."

"Although we certainly hope that changes," Dad interjected.

"Right. But we didn't want to pick something you'd hate, so we thought we'd just ask you what you would want?"

"And we're rich, so sky's the limit," Dad chuckled.

"It's really not necessary," Fox replied. "I was doing my job." He squeezed my hand as if to let me know I was much more than a job.

"We insist," my father exclaimed. "No objections."

"Within reason, obviously." Mom, ever the voice of practicality. "But yes, don't pick a keychain thinking you want to spare our pocketbook."

Fox chuckled.

I looked at Fox. "You deserve it. Do you have any idea what you'd want?"

"You know what?" His eyes roamed over my face. "I know *exactly* what I want."

"Wonderful." Mom clapped her hands. "What would you like?"

Fox kept his gaze steady on mine. "I'd like your daughter's hand in marriage."

My breath suspended in midair. What was he saying?

"I'm sorry?" Mom sputtered.

Fox broke eye contact with me and shifted in his seat to face my parents. "I'd like your blessing to marry your daughter. I'm fully aware she has to agree, but it would be wonderful if you were okay with our union."

"You barely know her," my father blustered, shock making his gray hairs seem prominent.

"Not true, sir. The parts that make Tori special? I know those secret places in her heart. And she knows mine. The adversity that built us but didn't break us."

I thought of the closeness we'd shared when he told me about his mom.

"She makes me want to show up and be present. The way she cares for her friends, goes full bravado even when she can't tell up from down. She makes me think about more than just myself. That's what loving her does to me. I'd argue that I know the essentials." His gaze slid over mine like a caress. "And the rest is a lifetime we'll discover together."

My pulse raced. Could I pass out from that romantic declaration as easily as the Hollywood starlets from the '50s?

"Tori?" Dad asked. "I thought the engagement was fake."

"It was." But Fox was what I wanted. *Who* I wanted. A lifetime with him. Security and love wrapped in a dark-chocolate package.

"And now?"

I blinked, trying to focus on what my dad was saying instead of getting lost in Fox's dreamy gaze. I cleared my throat. "Now my heart is involved."

"But sweetie," Mom objected. "You two haven't even known each other that long."

I rolled my eyes. "And you married Dad after two weeks of speed dating. Your words, not mine."

Mom pursed her lips, and I had to stifle a chuckle. We were too alike in a lot of aspects.

"That was a different time," Dad stated.

"Then you would go back and wait?"

He glared at me. "That's not what I said."

"But that's what you want me to do. Wait, when you didn't because you felt that marrying Mom was right."

"Are you saying that this thing between you two is right?" Dad gestured between us. "That you *know* with certainty he's for you?"

I slid my fingers through Fox's. "I've seen glimpses all along. Seen him in my dreams." I turned toward my parents. "And being with Fox, learning to love him, led me to God. How can that be wrong?"

"I hate it when you use logic." Mom pouted. "You know I want you to be happy, sweetie."

"Being with Fox makes me happy."

"Maybe you should wait." Dad held up a hand to stay my retort. "Not because I don't think he's upstanding, but you did just come out of an intense situation."

"Which only solidified my feelings. I wanted more before I was abducted, but fear kept me from saying so. And now I realize how foolish that was."

Fox squeezed my hand as he looked steadily toward my parents. "Will you give us your blessing?"

Mom turned toward Dad and they gazed at one another, using their wordless communication skills. Their ability to converse without speaking used to drive me crazy as a teen but was now my relationship goal.

Finally, they faced us.

My breath caught as I waited.

"We will," my father said.

Relief pulsed through me, and I squeezed Fox's hand tighter.

"Thank you." Fox voice deepened with emotion.

Mom nodded at him, but as she turned to me, she squealed and clapped her hands together. "That means we need to go dress shopping."

My mouth dropped open. "The wedding is next month!" I whirled toward Fox. "Did you want to pick a new date?"

"No." He leaned his forehead against mine. "That day is meant for us."

"Are you sure?" I whispered.

"Positive."

I kissed his cheek. "Then I'm going to scram and go dress shopping with my mother."

He kissed me. "Hurry back."

"You bet."

Mom laid a hand on my arm, impeding my steps toward the door.

"Yes?"

"You know you have to call the girls. They're not going to want to miss this."

"Are you sure? I'm perfectly fine with mother and daughter only time."

"Of course, sweetie. They're your best friends."

"Thank you." I threw my arms around her and squeezed.

Mom mentioned a reputable wedding shop, and I nodded in agreement as my thumbs flew across my cell screen.

T: MEET ME AT THE DRESS.

H: IS THERE SOMETHING YOU NEED

TO TELL US?

O: OMGEE!

I sent them a GIF of a woman in a wedding gown with the word *yes* flashing across the screen.

H: TORI!!!!

O: HE PROPOSED FOR REAL?

T: WE AGREED WE WANTED TO GET MARRIED FOR REAL. MOM'S TAKING ME DRESS SHOPPING. ON THE PHONE RIGHT NOW PROBABLY TRYING TO GET US SQUEEZED IN. SHE KNOWS THE OWNER.

Octavia sent a gif of Rachel and Phoebe from *Friends* jumping up and down.

H: WE'LL BE RIGHT THERE!

I turned toward Mom as she hung up her call. "Are we good?"

"Yes. They'll make sure everything goes smoothly."

"Thank you so much."

"Are you sure this is what you want to do?" The lines around Mom's eyes deepened as her blue-green irises searched mine.

"I'm positive. I know this is right." I could feel it down to the nerve endings in my toes. God had fought my battle. Had sent Fox to keep me safe and show me how great love could be.

Thank You. Thank You for everything.

For once, I didn't feel tied to societal expectations or even my parents'. But I did want them to genuinely be happy for me. I wouldn't change my mind, no matter how much they asked. Hopefully, they could come to accept this.

"I trust you."

"And you can trust Fox. He's the most…" My voice trailed

off, and my emotions clogged my throat. "He's the best, Mom." I held her hand. "In all your dreams for me, in wondering who'd I lose my heart to, realize he's the answer to that. I know my heart is safe with him. Not because he's perfect, but because he wants the best for me. Even if I don't want to hear it."

Tears filled Mom's eyes and she drew a shaky hand over her mouth. "Oh, sweetie, I'm so happy for you." She wrapped her arms around me, pressing me close. "So happy."

"Thank you," I whispered.

She pulled back. "Let's go get you the dress of your dreams."

"Yes!"

I PULLED THE SASH ON MY SILK ROBE TIGHTER AS I NERVOUSLY waited for the bridal consultant to come to my dressing room with a few gown choices. I'd told her I wanted something simple with a sweetheart neckline. I'd see what she brought back based off so little direction.

"Knock, knock." A rap of knuckles followed the pronouncement.

"Come in."

Judy smiled and walked in with four gowns. I rubbed my palms together as she placed them on the hooks.

"I have the perfect one to start with." She held up a dress with a mermaid silhouette.

I hung my robe up and stepped into the satin creation.

"This particular style will accentuate your figure wonderfully." She tugged on the dress as she zipped it up. The bodice had tiny bead work while the skirt flared out in undecorated tulle. It wasn't horrible, but I didn't love it. Not sure why she thought it would be perfect.

"Ready to show your family?"

"Sure." I smiled at her reflection in the mirror.

I walked out of the dressing room feeling like I was on the

runway of the most important fashion show of my life. The ladies oohed and aahed as I stepped up onto the platform. I spun around and stopped, facing them. "What do you think?"

"You don't love it," Holiday said.

"I don't."

"Then pass." Mom flung her hand in the air.

"Okay, onto the next one," Judy said.

After putting on the second dress, I was back in front of the girls. The bottom was covered with lace ruffles, but not a stitch of beading sparkled on the dress.

"No," they chorused.

I chuckled. "Don't need a moment to think about it?

"Not even."

I paraded in front of them in gown after gown. None of the designs were a hit. By the tenth dress, I was starting to get nervous. What if I couldn't find the perfect one? Was I wrong in going simple?

"Okay, dear, this one is it."

"Are you sure?"

"Just you wait and see. Step in."

I kept my eyes closed as she zipped me up. Before, I had eagerly watched the whole process of stuffing me in and zipping or buttoning me up. Now, I prayed I could say *this one*.

"Open."

My lids fluttered as I breathed in enough courage to inspect my reflection. I gasped. The sweetheart neckline was devoid of ornament. Well, the whole dress was. In a simple silk, the silhouette nipped in at the waist, hugged my hips, and then fluttered out in an A-line at the knees. I turned to peek at the back. A tiny row of buttons trailed down my spine.

"I love it."

"I told you we'd find *the one*. Now, let's go see how your

family reacts. I bet you anything your mom cries."

I grinned. "You're on."

But Ms. Judy was right. Tears sprang to Mom's eyes as Octavia gasped and Holiday's mouth dropped open.

"You look gorgeous, Tori." Holiday jumped up from the couch, taking me in. "Absolutely stunning. You look classy and in love all at the same time."

"I agree. It's perfect," Octavia said.

Mom sniffed through her tears while dabbing at her eyes.

"I guess it's safe to say she likes it." I chuckled and the ladies joined me.

"Now, let's help you with the accessories," Judy said.

A short while later, as Mom went to the counter to add the items we'd chosen, I looked at Holiday. "Why don't you try on something?"

"Oh, no, this is your day."

I rolled my eyes. "Please, like we never do group celebrations. Besides, you got engaged before me."

She bit her lip. "I don't know."

"Please?" I pleaded, bringing my hands up in a prayer motion underneath my chin.

"You really should, Hol." Octavia turned her big brown eyes on Holiday.

"Fine." She threw her hands up in the air.

We cheered and I went to tell Judy.

I sat down on the sofa between Mom and Octavia. "I'm so excited."

"Holiday will look beautiful in anything she tries on," Mom said.

"True. Who wants to guess what style she'll come out in?" I looked at my mom and then Tavia.

"Ball gown," Mom stated.

"Nah, I think sheath," Tavia countered.

"I think you're both wrong. I think she'll go for A-line."

Mom huffed. "Material?"

"Silk," Octavia shouted.

I chuckled. Thankfully, we had a private viewing room complete with champagne service, and no one else to hear us get a little noisy.

"Oops," she whispered.

"I'll say lace. Mom?" I turned toward her.

"Satin."

I nearly crowed with delight when Holiday walked out in a lace gown. Except I had to eat my victory, because the skirt of the ball gown would rival Cinderella's.

"You look beautiful," Mom said.

Holiday's nose scrunched up. "Thanks, Mrs. B, but I don't think I'm the ball gown type."

"Agreed," Tavia and I chorused. The gown swamped her.

She followed Judy out of the room, and I turned toward my mom. "Are you ready to gain a daughter-in-law?"

"Most definitely. I love you girls. I only wish I had another son for you, Tavia."

Octavia chuckled. "That's okay, Mrs. B. I have no time for men. Not if I'm going to dance again." Her voice trailed off.

I squeezed her hand. "You will. I'll pray it's so."

She leaned her head on my shoulder. "Thanks."

Holiday tried a few more gowns on, her nose wrinkling each time. But she amused us with a twirl before changing into another one. Finally, she came out grinning ear to ear. Mom gasped beside me.

I stared at the stunning dress on my best friend. It had a halter illusion neckline with a swirl of designs covering the beaded bodice. The rest of the light tulle material fell softly at her empire waistline.

"Oh, Holiday. Emmett will just melt." Mom started sniffing again, and I passed the tissues. "I'm so honored you'd let me be a part of this moment," she wailed.

My eyes teared up, as did Holiday's. My friend didn't have a mother to share this moment with. I got up and wrapped my arms around her. "I love you, Hol. I'm so glad we'll be sisters."

"Me too, girl." She squeezed me.

I stepped back as Judy came back with a lace veil. It flowed down Holiday's soft curls and stopped midleg. She looked amazing.

"It's gorgeous, Hol," Octavia said.

"Have you guys settled on a date?" Mom asked.

"We talked about it, but I'm waiting to hear from the label about my next tour. We don't want to get married in the middle of that craziness."

"Makes sense," I murmured.

As we walked out of the store, I turned to Mom and hugged her. "I'm going to catch a ride home with the girls."

"Of course. I imagine they want all the details from earlier."

"You know us too well."

"Enjoy yourself."

"Love you."

"Love you, Astoria."

I slid into the Town Car and squealed. "I can't believe we got dresses!" I turned to look at Octavia. "You're next, lady."

She shook her head. "No, ma'am." She patted her knee brace. "I have enough on my plate. I'm not looking to add anything else."

"Are you ready for surgery?"

Tavia shrugged. "If it lets me get back to dancing, yes."

My stomach twisted at the despondency in her voice. "You'll dance again, Tavia. I know it."

"But what if I'm no longer good enough to be the principal?"

"Would it matter so long as you could still dance for the company?" Holiday asked quietly.

I held my breath. It would have to hurt, going from being a principal to just another face in the troupe, but she would still be dancing. I searched Octavia as she mulled over Holiday's question.

"I honestly don't know."

Holiday reached for her hand and then held out her other to me. I slid mine against her palm.

"We should pray." Holiday looked at me for agreement.

"Definitely."

Holiday smiled and I bowed my head.

"Dear Lord, we ask that You would look after Octavia. Please heal her completely. Please help her get her dream back, God. In Jesus' name. Amen."

"Amen," I whispered.

Octavia sniffled. "Thank you."

TODAY'S SPA DAY WAS DIFFERENT THAN ANY WE'D HAD BEFORE. Holiday, Octavia, my mom, Miss Etta, Sasha, and I were getting the works for my evening wedding. Sasha kept squealing over every new pampering we received. Her phone had been practically glued to her hand so she could take pictures and post them later on Instagram. We'd posed with her in a couple of shots and given her permission to post already.

And I was happy to hear those girls had stopped bullying her.

Holiday and Octavia loved Sasha. And Miss Etta loved everyone. At first, she'd protested when I invited her to the spa day. Thought she was too old and didn't want to ruin our fun.

"Miss Etta, my day wouldn't be possible without the love you showed Fox. Say you'll come. Plus, my mom will be there."

"You twisted my arm."

Which is how she found herself getting curls put into her gray do. Once our hair was done, we'd be moving on to makeup. Anticipation coiled in my middle. I couldn't wait to walk down the aisle and say *I do.*

I had asked Holiday if she was upset that we were marrying before her and Emmett. She quickly put my fears to rest. I glanced at her. Her hairdresser looked like a robot, wrist rotating as she put loose curl after loose curl in Holiday's hair.

The girls—Holiday, Octavia, and Sasha—were going to wear identical rose-gold gowns. The bodice was beaded rose gold but had a rose overlay in a twisted halter to match the skirt that fell to the floor. They looked great in them, and I couldn't wait until the ceremony.

I'm going to be Mrs. Marcel Fox! "Do you suppose I'll have to start calling him Marcel, since we're about to get married?"

Holiday's mouth dropped. "You don't already?"

I shrugged. "I did once. When I told him I loved him."

A chorus of awws echoed through the room. I shook my head at the sappy ladies but couldn't keep the smile off my own face.

"I think it's cute. But you might want to call him Marcel more often," Octavia suggested.

"Can I call you Foxy Lady when you marry?" Holiday asked.

Miss Etta chuckled, and Sasha covered her face.

"I'll take that as a no."

"Not if you don't want me calling you Lady Waldorf," I retorted.

Holiday shuddered. "Sounds like something out of a Gothic novel. Things never end well in those."

We finished with hair and makeup, then headed to the bridal suite the Loft Garden had set aside for us to use as a dressing room. Mom and Sasha snapped picture after picture as Holiday and Octavia took care buttoning my million buttons. Tavia started at the top, since she couldn't kneel. Finally, they were done.

I was ready.

Ready to become Mrs. Marcel Fox. Ready to say *I do.* Ready to live the good life God had in store for me.

———

HOLIDAY CROONED OF A LOVE WORTH WAITING FOR AS I WALKED down the aisle, my dad struggling to keep his tears at bay. My gaze glued to Fox and his to mine. As my father handed me over, Fox whispered, "I'll take good care of her, sir."

"You've already proven you can. Don't let the hard moments make you doubt, son."

Now I was going to have to blink back tears. But as my hand slid into Fox's, the world righted and I only felt like smiling.

"I'm not calling you Marcel," I whispered.

"Fine by me, Princess."

I bit the inside of my cheek to keep from laughing outright. I loved this man.

We exchanged vows, and when he slid my ring back on my finger, tears sprang to my eyes. I hadn't seen the beautiful aquamarine since the day of the cake tasting. Now my hand no longer felt naked. I smiled up at Fox as the officiant finished the ceremony and pronounced us man and wife.

"You may now kiss the bride."

"It's about time," Fox murmured. He cradled the back of my head and I slid my hands up his arms. Our lips met and a fresh wave of awareness filled me. We were married. Husband and wife. Together.

He pulled back, and the sound of clapping slowly penetrated my ears.

"I love you, Marcel."

"I love you too, Tori."

"Are you ready for those dreams to become reality?"

"More than you can imagine."

We grinned and walked down the aisle, hand in hand.

EPILOGUE

OCTAVIA

My breath shuddered as I pushed down the sobs gathering like a storm in my chest. A ruptured ACL. How unfair. I stared at my knee, covered in a brace. Any moment now, the physical therapist would make his visit and bring forth the torture.

But it would be worth all the pain and hard work to get back to dancing. To breathe without the constant pressure constricting my chest. Because life without dancing…

I swallowed back another sob. I needed to rely on my strength. I wasn't out of shape. The doctor said my daily fitness routine would aid my healing, but he couldn't promise that I'd return to ballet.

"Why me, Lord?" My whisper sounded flat even to my ears.

My faith felt nonexistent, and God's presence…I didn't know what that felt like any longer.

Tori was married. Holiday engaged. I might as well have been all alone in our five-story home. "Where are you, God? Why have you left me?"

And how did I move forward? How could I come back

from this? Because despite the exercises I'd been doing since my attack, I felt no better. Granted, my surgery wasn't until next week, but still. I wanted to be healed, and I wanted it right now.

All the prayers I'd uttered since that first diagnosis seemed to have fallen on deaf ears. I was all alone, and no one was around to help me.

I pushed my shoulders back. I would have to rely on myself. To pull from the will power that had made me a principal ballerina. A title that only one other African American woman could claim. Adversity had built me. I couldn't let it make me crumble now.

But maybe I'd allow myself a few more tears until the therapist came.

SNEAK PEAK

Preorder Now

The Price of Dreams

By
Toni Shiloh

I

I EXHALED AND MOVED INTO A *FOUETTÉ EN TOURNANT EN dehors.* Using my right leg to extend and come back in at a triangle, I thrust my body around in a full turn. Muscle memory immediately propelled my legs through a *glissade* and into fourth position before making the transition into a *grand jeté.* I leapt into the air, exhilarating in the freedom of the movement as the music's crescendo stirred the scene to one of joy and exultation.

My partner moved to my side and swooped me into a fish dive, my face dangerously close to the floor. No panic—only trust resided, because we'd done this sequence over and over and over, each time perfecting the movements. The constant training I'd put my muscles and mind through commanded my limbs, every inch of me presented to the audience with precision.

Ballet was the ultimate visual art, and I was completely aware that my physical form embodied the passion and story the choreographers and musicians wanted to tell, letting the audience in on the secrets of love and heartache, overcoming and triumphant happiness.

I bent at the waist, my right knee kneeling on the stage in

a *révérence*, or curtsy, as the music came to an end. The crowd rose to their feet with a roar of applause. But the ovation wasn't meant for me. Not for me alone, anyway. It took more than one person to pull off a performance. Every production required a massive team effort all made to look seamless and fluid.

I blinked as the memory faded and reality set in.

I, Octavia Ricci, am a principal ballerina for the City Ballet Company. Or rather, I *was*. Now the only dances I could perform were those in my memory. Last month, I'd received the call informing me that another ballerina would take my starring position as principal ballerina for the performances my body could no longer execute. One attack from a stalker and my knee had failed me. Not *my* stalker, but my best friend's, Tori Bell.

Wait, she's Tori Fox now.

Anyhow, the assault left me with a ruptured ligament in my knee and a note of warning from the doctor that I may never dance again.

Never dance again?

Those words made no sense. I couldn't comprehend them, though I lay here in a hospital bed recovering from anterior cruciate ligament (ACL) reconstruction surgery. The doctor had given me three options prior to cutting me open. Number one: they could use a donor graft, taking an ACL from a deceased individual and grafting the tissues into my body.

I shuddered at the thought every time it sprang to mind. *Ew!* Although the easiest option, it wouldn't guarantee my return to the dance I loved so much.

Option two had been to graft tissue from my patella. This choice made me less queasy. However, I would have been left with a partial knee cap. Kind of needed that for stability in dancing. The last route proved to be the most difficult and came with the longest recovery time. Yet picking this choice gave me the best chance of returning to ballet at the same level I had performed before. After gaining my consent, the surgeon had taken part of my hamstring to reconstruct a new ACL.

Now my left leg burned with pain.

I shifted in the hospital bed and moaned, then studied the whiteboard in my room where the nurse had kindly written the times I was scheduled to receive another dose of pain medication. The initial narcotics had torn my stomach apart, leaving me hovering over a pink plastic container and needing new sheets, since I'd missed the bowl the first time my insides revolted.

Now I was relegated to nonnarcotic pain medication and anti-inflammatories, alternating between the two to keep my pain under control. I pressed the nurse icon on my remote and waited for someone at the station to respond. A voice spoke through the room intercom system and told me my nurse would be right in.

I sighed. Hopefully, the doctor would let me go home tomorrow. For some reason, he wanted me to stay the night for observation. Which, granted, if he hadn't made the order, I never would have realized the awful affect the narcotic drugs had on my body.

Two taps rapped on the door and then it swung open. "Afternoon, Ms. Ricci. Time for some pain meds?" the nurse asked.

"Please, Dianne." I smiled at the petite RN. She was a sweetheart and didn't deserve any bad attitude from me. It was a struggle to remember my manners through the haze of pain though.

She handed me a measuring cup with two tablets in it and passed the hospital mug full of water. "Here you go, sweetie." She pushed her glasses up the bridge of her nose.

"Thank you." I downed the meds and handed her the empty cup and water.

"Very good. I looked at your chart and your physical therapist will be in soon."

I bit back a groan. Wasn't it bad enough I'd already been tortured by him prior to surgery? Apparently having PT before surgery was supposed to help me heal faster afterward. All I knew was it was torturous, and now that I'd had the surgery, I expected the level of pain and annoyance to increase exponentially.

"All right."

"Rest until he comes, dear."

"Okay." I offered a smile, even though I knew resting would be impossible.

I hadn't slept well with all the comings and goings. You'd think the meds would've helped, but the pain in my leg and the thought of never dancing again kept me from sleeping soundly. In fact, I hadn't slept a full eight hours since the attack. But I would squeeze my eyes shut and try.

In the past, I would've sung a gospel or Christian song to lull me to sleep, but since my ACL rupture, God had been quiet. Had left me out in the cold, alone, without a word from Him. The Bible said that He would never forsake us, but the silence, the empty void that greeted me when I called out to Him, said otherwise.

Didn't it?

"Therapy time."

I blinked at the voice that intruded on my thoughts. Had it been a half hour already? I glanced at the clock and then at my physical therapist—Dr. Noah Wright.

"Good afternoon, Octavia." His gaze assessed me then shifted away.

Noah always seemed uncomfortable saying my name, which was odd, because he'd asked that I use his instead of calling him Dr. Wright. Maybe being on a first name basis with me was too personable for him? Did other clients insist on being called by their first name? I wasn't a formal person, so it made no sense to be referred to as Ms. Ricci. Or maybe that was my way of distancing myself from my father.

I stared at the green-eyed doctor. His brown hair was always mussed in multiple directions. Was he one of those men who ran his fingers through his hair when stressed, or did he simply refuse to use a brush?

But that wasn't what gave me pause every time he came around. It was his quiet demeanor that promised he'd listen to every word you had to say. Those penetrating eyes that seemed to see deep into my soul to the pain I kept stuffing down.

"Good afternoon, Noah." My voice was quiet, hesitant. Because, truthfully, I was still trying to work out this strange dynamic between us. Sure, he was personable and friendly at times, but I always got the sense he was holding back. And I really wanted to know why.

Maybe my fame threw him off. Ever since I'd received the position of principal ballerina, I'd been plastered all over the newsstands. Though, not as much as my best friends, Tori and Holiday. For one, Tori was a supermodel, recently married, and a kidnapping survivor. Holiday was a platinum-recording pop singer engaged to Tori's brother, who also happened to be a Pulitzer Prize-winning photographer.

Next to them, my notoriety seemed tame. But being one of two African American principal ballerinas in America—formerly, now—gave me some limelight next to Misty Copeland, the other African American principal. Being the daughter of winemaker Donovan Ricci put me in other elite circles—because everyone wanted a bottle of Ricci Winery's finest.

Nah. Why would an educated doctor, a specialist in sports injuries, be intimidated by me? I scoffed under my breath. "What's the plan today, doc?"

He pierced me with his eyes.

I corrected myself. "Noah."

"I actually just want to do some light stretching. We don't want your leg to tense or tighten up more." He smiled at me. He always seemed more self-assured when talking medicine.

I had to admit, he was good looking for a white guy. I'd never dated a Caucasian before. Not because I hated that part of myself, but because the world saw me as Black, and I knew from my parents' own experience that interracial relationships only caused headaches.

Not that I dated a lot anyway. I'd been too involved with ballet to give my love to any man, white or Black.

"We need to give your leg and knee good feedback." Noah's soft voice interrupted my musings. "I'll do a light massage so your nerve receptors will relax some and give your body the message everything will be okay."

I met his gaze, trying to focus on his words and ignore the pain and random thoughts floating in my head. "Okay."

He pushed back the blanket, keeping my right leg underneath for a veil of modesty and propriety. I looked down at my other leg wrapped in gauze.

"Does it hurt?"

"Yes."

He nodded and placed his hands behind my calf. "How's this?"

"No pain there."

"Good. You relax and let me just slowly work your leg up."

I nodded and closed my eyes, inhaling and exhaling slow and steady breaths. The fluidity of ballet had introduced me to controlled breathing a long time ago. The more I could relax, the better stretch Noah would be able to give my left leg.

"Octavia?"

"Yes?" I cracked an eyelid at the cautious tone in his voice and found Noah staring at me. Was something wrong? Both of my eyes sprang open.

"What do you want out of your therapy sessions?"

Huh? He'd already asked me this when we first met in October, hadn't he? "I want to dance again. You know this."

A half smile curved his lips. "I know, but at what level? Recreational? Professional? Do you want me to take it easy on you or push you, knowing I'll stop before your body reaches its limits?"

My thigh tensed as he hit a painful area.

"Relax," he instructed as he moved my leg up, extending my fiery hamstring.

I purposely blew out a breath, my brow furrowing. "I need to be a principal ballerina again. I do *not* need coddling, *Dr.* Wright."

His puppy-dog eyes met mine then bounced away. "Ouch. I didn't mean to tick you off." He held my leg steady, sustaining the stretch. "I want to know your goals so that I can ensure we meet them."

Oh. I bit my lip, studying him. "I apologize."

He averted his eyes and lowered my leg back down. "How does it feel?"

I took a mental body assessment, much like the ones I'd do after practicing or performing. "It hurts less."

"Good. Positive feedback will help in your recovery, but we will push you so you can get back to center stage." He held out his hand, finally meeting my gaze. "Deal?"

I slipped my hand in his, ignoring the way my heart seemed to sigh at the warmth of his touch.

Shaking his hand always produced this effect.

And I always ignored it. "Deal."

ACKNOWLEDGMENTS

Another book, hooray! I love each of my book babies and each one had a group of people to help me along. I'd like to first thank my critique partners for being the first set of eyes on a rough draft and helping my story shine. I couldn't do what I do without Andrea Boyd, Jaycee Weaver, and Sarah Monzon. I love you guys!

I also have to give a huge thanks to my beta readers. Ashley Espie, Marylin Furumasu, Carrie Schmidt, Ebos Aifuobhokhan, and Vicky Sluiter. Your feedback was invaluable, and I can't thank you enough for taking the time to read through my manuscript on such a tight deadline.

And of course I can't forget my editor extraordinaire Katie Donovan. Thank you so much for all of your hard work and for working on this series so quickly. You're the best!

Special shout out to Julie Rush for the Enchantment magazine name and to my readers for buying my books time and again. You bless me immensely and I can't thank you enough for making my writing journey so awesome.

Last but not least, my husband and kids. Thank you for giving me the time to write and zone out. I love y'all!

ABOUT THE AUTHOR

Toni Shiloh is a wife, mom, and multi-published Christian contemporary romance author. She writes to bring her Savior glory and to learn more about His grace.

Her novel, *Grace Restored*, was a 2019 Holt Medallion finalist and *Risking Love* is a 2020 Selah Award finalist. She is a member of the American Christian Fiction Writers (ACFW) and president of the Virginia Chapter.

You can find her on her website at http://tonishiloh.com. Signup for her Book News newsletter at http:// eepurl.com/gcMfqT.

More Books by Toni Shiloh

Short Novels

The Maple Run Series

Buying Love

Finding Love

Enduring Love

Risking Love

Faith & Fortune Series

The Trouble With Love

NOVELS

Freedom Lake Series
Returning Home
Grace Restored
Finally Accepted

Novellas
A Life to Live
A Sidelined Christmas
Deck the Shelves
A Proxy Wedding